Werewolf Breeding Academy

Part 1-3

Beatrix Arden

Images: © Canva © Can Stock Photo/Forewer

Author Website: beatrixarden.com

Other Hot Stories by Beatrix Arden

Chained Omega

Werewolf Breeding Academy

You're my Omega

Omega Harem Lost

The Village Omega

Alpha Hates Alpha

Omega Fills Omega

Subscribe to Beatrix Arden new release notifications!

Get notified of new stories by email and get free ebooks.

sub.beatrixarden.com

CONTENTS

WARNING

This book is dark werewolf smut written for adults 18+. It contains multiple erotic scenes and unhealthy relationships that would not work in the real world.

WEREWOLF
BREEDING
ACADEMY

BY BEATRIX ARDEN

CHAPTER ONE

What the....

Riley could barely believe the scene before her.

Two students were going at it in the middle of the school lawn.

They were mostly clothed, but the woman was on her hands and knees as a burly guy pounded into her from behind.

The pace was brutal, but the woman didn't care, letting out loud screams like no one was watching.

"Yes Brodie! Yes!" she cried out in ecstasy. "Put your big strong wolf babies inside me!"

It was like watching a car crash.

Riley quickly looked away with horror, but the slapping of his dick echoed throughout the courtyard.

What shocked her most was that no one seemed to care.

Everyone was merrily going about their day as though two people weren't bumping uglies in public.

A group of students were casually hanging out nearby, two girls were playing badminton, and a teacher was herding young people into the red brick school building.

Riley looked to her friend Wanda for help, but the tall woman was still happily pointing to various buildings as though the shameless exhibition-ists didn't exist.

"And over there are the dorms," said Wanda. "And then the cafeteria is over there."

"*Doesn't it bother you?*" Riley hissed, nervously threading her fingers through her long black hair.

"Well.. they are far apart," said Wanda.

"Not the buildings," Riley snapped back. "*Them*." She subtly tilted her head in the direction of the couple.

Wanda stared at Riley blankly for a moment.

"Oh, them." Wanda laughed when she finally caught on. "You know what new couples are like."

No! Riley wanted to scream. Nobody ever screwed each other in front of the teachers at her old school.

"I forget that people aren't like that on the outside," Wanda said. "Here it's perfectly fine. So you don't need to worry about it."

Riley's dark eyes almost bulged out of their sockets. She knew that werewolves were a bit eccentric, but this was far beyond her expectations.

A month earlier, Riley would have laughed if anyone told her that werewolves were real.

She was traveling the country in her van, picking up farm work here and there, but then she went out for a leak and got attacked by a werewolf.

Her last human memory was bleeding out on the grass as her body slowly transformed.

The next few months were a blur as her new wolf body pranced around the mountains, slowly forgetting that she'd ever been human.

Riley probably would have spent the rest of her life hunting down rabbits and peeing on trees, if Wanda and Wanda's father hadn't found her.

They managed to snap Riley out of her trance and help her change back into a human, but it was still touch and go.

Riley found it difficult to control the wild animal that had firmly lodged itself into her brain.

She hoped that the academy could help her live a semi-normal life, but now she wasn't sure.

Wanda continued merrily talking about the school like Riley wasn't having an internal panic attack.

Wanda's dark braids swayed behind her with each step, and her gold gel nails glittered in the sun.

Unlike Riley, Wanda had been a werewolf since birth, so she could control her inner animal with ease. She made everything look easy.

Riley doubted that she would ever be a half decent werewolf. All she wanted was to control it enough to re-enter human society without biting someone's head off.

Riley followed Wanda through the courtyard into the school building.

The red brick exterior and yellowing wallpaper reminded Riley of the Christian camps that her mother used to offload her to.

The school was large enough to accommodate a few hundred students. Most of them were college age.

Other than a bunch of wolves dashing down the hall, it didn't appear too different from a regular school.

Riley and Wanda stopped halfway through a quiet corridor, far removed from the other classrooms.

A piece of paper with the words *new wolves* was taped to a battered wooden door.

"This is you," said Wanda. "I'll catch you at lunch."

"Are you sure that I can't go with you?" Riley nervously tugged on her shirt sleeve. "I know that your classes are for real werewolves, but perhaps they won't notice me there."

"Don't worry." Wanda smiled. "You'll be fine. I promise that these guys won't bite......much."

Riley's jaw dropped open.

Wanda let out a laugh. "I was just joking, okay. How come you always take everything so seriously?"

"Please don't joke with me," Riley moaned. "I can never tell when you're serious or just making shit up."

"You'll be fine." Wanda took hold of Riley's shoulders and gave her a gentle shove into the classroom. "Go get them, Tiger."

It wasn't as bad as Riley expected. There were about a dozen students, all looking as equally confused and disoriented as her.

There was one guy furiously scratching himself, a girl curled up in the corner, and another girl covered in golden fur like she was half-way through a transformation.

Riley took a seat next to a guy wearing a baseball hat and hoodie. There were headphones shoved into his ears, and he kept flinching like a nervous tic. He nodded his head as a silent greeting.

I can deal with this, Riley thought.

The moment that thought entered her head, the sound of lips smacking echoed throughout the room.

Riley turned to see a couple furiously making out at the desk behind hers. The girl was practically in the guy's lap as she tried to eat his face.

Riley crossed her arms and looked to the front of the room, trying to block out the noise.

Were all werewolves shit at controlling themselves?

Riley felt relieved when a scruffy blonde teacher entered the room.

His lower face was concealed by a bushy beard, and he was carrying a large mug of coffee.

He wrote *Mr. Bites* on the board in large letters, then turned to face them.

"Good morning class," he said brightly.

No one returned his greeting.

The girl in the corner began muttering to herself, and the couple behind Riley continued making out.

"I'm sure that this is a new and confusing time for you all," said Mr. Bites. "As young adults who grew up on the outside, your brains haven't fully developed to accommodate your new animal instincts. You risk losing control and becoming nothing more than mindless wolves."

Riley tried to focus on his words, but it was impossible to concentrate.

The couple were still violently making out, except the girl straddled her partner's lap, grinding herself against his groin while making exaggerated moans.

"Yeah, baby," the guy huffed. "Can't wait to shove my big cock inside you."

Riley wanted to smash her head against the desk. She couldn't believe that the teacher wasn't doing anything.

Was he blind and deaf? How could he concentrate with them being so loud?

Riley was contemplating raising her hand, when the teacher finally said something.

Mr. Bites tossed an eraser in the couple's direction, hitting the guy on the forehead.

"Davis," he scolded. "What have you been told about breeding in class?"

Finally! Riley thought. *There's no way that even werewolves could get away with that sort of shit.*

"Keep it down," huffed the guy.

"Exactly," said Mr. Bites without batting an eyelid. "And keep your eyes to the front. You wouldn't want to miss anything important."

"Yeah, I got you." Davis repositioned his partner so that she was sitting in his lap, soft arse rubbing against his hard cock. "I'll make sure to keep it nice and quiet."

What the fuck! Riley wanted to scream at them.

What sort of messed up world had she just arrived in?

Riley groaned and tried to keep her eyes to the front, but it was impossible to block them out.

The girl bent over the desk as Davis pulled up her skirt, exposing her naked arse. He rubbed his groin against the soft skin before pulling down his track pants to expose his rock hard cock.

Without an ounce of hesitation, he slipped his erection straight inside her dripping pussy, letting out a moan.

His girlfriend hissed as it buried deep inside her.

Davis huffed as he slowly slid is cock in and out, trying his best to remain quiet.

"And make sure that you come fully inside her this time," said Mr. Bites. "You don't want to be cleaning the floor again. Do you, Davis?"

"No, Sir," Davis huffed. "Gonna fill her up. Gonna fill her up good."

This was not what Riley signed up for.

Not once during all of Wanda's lectures about werewolf life, did she mention that students would be fucking in class.

Riley wanted to walk out, but they were half way up a mountain and miles from the closest town. Even if she convinced someone to drive her back to civilization, she was still broke and homeless. All her things had been impounded and her family still thought she was dead.

She had nowhere else left to go.

Riley shoved her fingers in her ears and tried her best to read the teacher's lips.

She was trapped in this nuthouse.

CHAPTER TWO

Riley was miserable by the time lunch arrived. She thought that Davis and his girlfriend would quit after they both got off, but they were soon back at it like a pair of horny dogs, using the desks and chairs around them like props in a bad porno.

The teacher did nothing to stop them.

Instead, he encouraged Davis to try different positions like it was part of the lesson plan.

"Make sure that she cums too," said Mr. Bites while casually taking a sip of coffee. "It's better for fertilization."

"Right. On it," said Davis while pumping his hips.

He reached down to rub his girlfriend's clit, making her tremble and pulse around his swollen dick.

"Yes! Yes!" she cried with such vigor that Riley wanted to rip her ears off.

Some of her classmates couldn't take it either.

A fight broke out between Davis and the girl covered in fur.

Mr. Bites broke them apart, but then lectured the class on werewolf mating habits like they didn't know what sex was.

Please kill me, Riley thought as Mr. Bites drew werewolf dicks on the board. *Please kill me now.*

She sadly made her way to the cafeteria at lunch, regretting all her life decisions.

She should have just headed straight off to college instead of taking a gap year.

If she'd stayed away from forests and nature, she could have been studying at a normal school with normal students instead of trapped in an exhibitionist's paradise.

The cafeteria was a large room full of long benches. The students sat in close-knit groups like they were still in high school.

The staff handed out pre-made trays full of meat and vegetables. The smell of rabbit and deer made Riley's mouth water.

She took a tray and searched the room for Wanda.

Her friend was laughing with another guy at the back of the room, empty plates stacked up before them.

He was broad with light brown skin and black hair that had been woven into dreadlocks. He was wearing a white tank top that showed off his large upper arms.

Wanda spotted Riley and waved her over. "Hey! How was it?"

"Terrible." Riley placed her tray down and took a seat. "Everyone was traumatized and this couple wouldn't stop banging."

"Better than last year then?" laughed the guy.

"Better?" said Riley. "How could last year have been any worse?"

"This one girl kept trying to bite everyone. They had to sedate her."

"At least there's no one like that," sighed Riley.

"Don't worry," said the guy. "They're probably just nervous. The real crazies will start showing soon."

Riley gagged.

"This is my cousin Tommy," said Wanda.

"Charmed," Tommy said with a large grin that showed off rows of perfect white teeth.

"Nice to meet you," Riley said with a nod.

She took a bite of her steak, trying her best to ignore a couple going at it at the table in front of them.

Riley winced. "Doesn't anyone get a room here?"

"Why should they?" Tommy shrugged. "It's all perfectly natural."

"Every living animal does it," Wanda added. "You don't see them trying to hide it."

"But what if she gets pregnant?" said Riley.

"Then she'll have a baby," said Tommy.

"Yeah, but what about school?" asked Riley.

"The elders will raise them," said Tommy.

"The elders love children," said Wanda.

"They're always pressuring us to have as many kids as possible," said Tommy.

"They keep talking about creating some grand werewolf society," said Wanda.

"It was their idea to make schools like this," said Tommy. "To learn more about our kind and mate as much as possible."

"Gotta make sure that everyone has a baby when spring rolls around," said Wanda.

Their words were so outlandish that it took Riley a moment to process them.

Then it hit her.

She was trapped in a strategic fuck fest.

It made sense. The students screwing everywhere. The lack of protection. The way that her own teacher egged Davis on.

"You realize what this place is, right?" Riley whispered, glancing over her shoulder. "They've shoved you all together and encourage you to have sex so that you'll make more kids for them."

"Maybe," Wanda said, like it wasn't a big deal. "I never thought of that before."

"Nobody seems to mind." Tommy shrugged.

"How can that not bother you?" Riley asked. "They're using you as baby machines."

"I mean....giving birth the first time was tough," said Wanda. "But it got a lot easier after the second."

Riley hoped that Wanda was joking. "You don't seriously have kids, right?"

"Of course I do," Wanda laughed. "Don't you?"

"No. You never told me that you have children," said Riley.

"I haven't?"

"No."

"But I thought that we talked about it."

"No, you haven't said anything."

"They live with my grandmother, so I don't see them that often."

"Elis is getting pretty big," said Tommy. "Last time I was there he was doing a good job at keeping up with the twins."

"Twins!" Riley exclaimed. "Wanda, how many do you have?"

"Three," Wanda replied.

"But you're only twenty!"

"I know right?" said Wanda. "My grandmother had five by now. She keeps pestering me to have another baby this spring."

"My grandfather offered me a hundred dollars for every baby I father this year," said Tommy.

"Nice," said Wanda. "I wish my parents weren't such cheapskates."

Unbelievable, Riley thought to herself.

They were both clearly brainwashed.

This werewolf sex cult was more messed up than she imagined.

"I could hook you up with some friends of mine," said Wanda. "I heard that Andy is pretty fertile. He must have at least twenty kids by now."

"I'm fine," said Riley. "I don't mind being single."

"But don't you want a baby in the spring?" asked Tommy.

"No, no," Riley nervously laughed. "I'm too broke for kids."

"You could send the baby to your parents," said Wanda.

Riley was certain that her parents would have a heart attack if she sent them a werewolf child, not to mention all the lectures she'd have to endure for getting pregnant so carelessly.

"My parents aren't really the type to help with things like that," said Riley.

"Oh." Wanda looked taken back like she hadn't thought it was possible. "Well...that's too bad."

A crash echoed behind them.

Riley turned to see several metal trays on the floor.

A gangly student with freckles was frantically trying to stack them back into a pile.

Standing before him was a pale guy with short blonde hair and piercing blue eyes. His cheek bones were well defined and he was dressed in a brand name jacket and sneakers.

There was nothing particularly unique about him, but he drew Riley's attention like a roaring flame.

She pressed her thighs together as a jolt of pleasure shocked through her core.

Him...

He was accompanied by a thin blonde girl who looked like she'd just sucked a lemon, and two large burly guys in tight shirts.

"Watch where you're going, half-breed," the blonde guy sneered and flipped the trays out of the student's hand, sending them crashing back to the floor.

His group walked away laughing. They sat down at a table full of equally blond haired blue eyed students. All silent and stoic like they'd never been taught how to smile.

Wanda followed Riley's line of sight. "Oh, the purists. They're always like that."

"Purists?" Riley felt rattled. She had to force the words out of her mouth.

"Their families have all been werewolves for centuries," said Tommy. "They think that it makes them better than the rest of us."

"Everyone calls them *The Master Race*," said Wanda. "But they take it as a compliment."

"You should stay clear of them," said Tommy. "They tend to pick on students who used to be human."

"Oh," said Riley.

"Don't worry," said Wanda. "They don't like me either because my mother is human. Just don't draw attention to yourself and they should leave you alone."

Riley nodded while munching on a fry. She resisted the overpowering urge to look in their direction.

All she had to do was keep her head down and remain unnoticed.

It couldn't be too hard.

CHAPTER THREE

Riley had more class after lunch.

Mr. Bites led them out to a patch of woods at the back of the school.

The girl who was in the corner soon found refuge behind some bushes, and Davis and his girlfriend were at it again.

They were screwing against a tree like they didn't just have an hour lunch break to get it out of their system.

Davis noticed Riley's angry glares in their direction. He was immune to her look of disgust.

"Yeah, you like that, huh?" Davis huffed while looking straight at Riley. "Come join us, you exotic beauty."

"No babe, not again," his girlfriend whined. "You promised no more threesomes."

"Can't help it," Davis groaned with a rock of his hips. "How can I deny anyone this pleasure maker?"

Riley quickly moved away.

"Hey," she asked a classmate wearing headphones. "Do you think I could borrow one of those?"

The guy shook his head like he didn't want to risk hearing Davis for a second.

Mr. Bites clapped his hands together to grab their attention.

"Today we'll practice turning into wolves," he said. "So everyone strip your clothes so we can get started."

Fuck no, Riley thought.

Luckily most of the class seemed to think the same thing.

One guy pulled his shirt over his head, but then stopped when no one else started stripping.

"There's no way that I'm getting naked in front of you!" one girl snapped.

"Would you feel better if I was also naked?" asked Mr. Bites.

"No way!" the girl snapped back. "I don't want to see old man dong."

"Okay," Mr. Bites nervously laughed. "Looks like we got ourselves another *clothes on* kinda group. I can work with that."

Riley breathed a sigh of relief.

"Natasha!" Mr. Bites called out to the girl covered in fur. "Since you're already half transformed, why don't you go first?"

With a growl, Natasha moved to the front of the group. She closed her eyes and began to hum.

"Now just relax and let your inner wolf take control," said their teacher. "Easy does it."

With the cracking of bones, Natasha's form began to change, morphing into a large wolf with golden fur.

She let out a long howl, then dashed straight into the forest, disappearing out of sight.

"Okaaay," Mr. Bites said like he didn't expect that to happen. "Why don't the rest of you have a go?"

All around Riley, her classmates tried transforming, morphing into wolves and ripping their clothes.

"Great job, everyone," said Mr. Bites. "Why don't you have a go, Ann?"

"No way," a petite girl snapped back while picking her nails. "Do you have any idea how much this dress is worth?"

"Maybe later then," said Mr. Bites. "How about you, Riley?"

Riley nodded. She slipped off her jacket, placing it on the ground beside her.

She closed her eyes and visualized turning into a wolf, just like Wanda taught her, but a familiar chill trickled down her spine.

What if she couldn't turn back?

Riley had spent months in fear, trapped in a strange body with no idea why, slowly losing her mind to the monster inside.

She never wanted to feel that again.

Being a wolf was terrifying, no matter how many times she was assured that practice was the only way to get it under control.

Riley clenched her fists to stop herself from shaking.

"Not to worry," Mr. Bites said with a friendly pat on her back. "Even the slow students get there eventually."

His words made her feel worse.

Riley sighed and sat down on a rock, watching the chaos unfold around her.

It was a shit show.

One girl was sobbing because she could transform only her hand, and another switched back to find her clothing in tatters.

A skinny guy was prancing around naked like he had no problem with their teacher's no clothing request, while another two students started screwing each other in wolf form.

Davis caught sight of them and started transforming into a wolf too, until his girlfriend screamed and pushed him away.

Their teacher didn't seem bothered by the insanity before him.

Riley could only assume that the man had seen far worse.

"Great job guys," Mr. Bites said. "Really making progress."

Riley rolled her eyes.

She caught hints of Wanda's scent on the wind.

But there was something else.

An alluring aroma that made her mouth prickle.

Riley got to her feet and searched for the source, discovering a set of concrete courts on the other side of the trees.

A group of students were playing volleyball.

Wanda was among them, dressed in a T-shirt and shorts as she tried to bounce the ball to her fellow students.

She dove for the ball, but another guy knocked her out of the way, sending them both crashing to the ground.

It was the same blonde guy who Riley saw at lunch.

He was dressed in a short T-shirt that showed off his well defined upper arms. His hair was tousled and beads of sweat ran down his forehead.

Just like before, Riley's body began to react, urging her closer.

Go to him... hissed a voice in her mind.

It took all of Riley's energy not to move.

"What the fuck, Elijah," one of his classmates said. "We're on the same team."

Elijah looked taken back, but he quickly composed himself.

"It was the half-breed who got in my way," he snapped.

"Whatever man," said the classmate. "Just don't do it again."

Wanda quickly got to her feet. Other than a few scratches, she looked mostly unharmed.

Normally Riley would have been more concerned for her friend, but she couldn't take her eyes off Elijah.

Just the sight of him caused an uncomfortable pulsing between her legs.

Elijah moved back into position, but then paused to sniff the wind, eyes almost bulging out of their sockets.

He quickly spun around, looking straight at Riley.

He froze, mouth gaping open.

It felt like the air had been sucked from Riley's lungs.

Her heart pounded in her chest as she struggled to breathe.

Him...

But then the moment was over.

Elijah let out a growl and stormed off the court.

"Mr. Brant!" a teacher yelled out, but Elijah didn't answer, continuing to walk away.

What the fuck was that?

Riley was overcome by a strange sense of loss.

She felt disappointed even though they had only looked at each other.

Was it another weird wolf thing that she'd have to deal with from now on? Was she going to experience hot flushes everytime that she saw a good looking guy?

Riley moved back to her class while massaging her forehead.

"Okay guys!" Mr. Bites called out, voice calm despite nervously running a hand through his hair. "Let's give it one more go before wrapping it up for today."

As much as Riley tried, she couldn't erase the memory of Elijah's sweat soaked body from her mind.

He was clearly strong and powerful. Those large hands would feel divine against her naked skin.

And the way that he looked at her.

It was like he imprinted himself into her brain.

Riley shivered as fur sprouted from her skin.

Her bones broke and realigned themselves, nose and jaw extending to form a snout. Her hands morphed into paws, and sharp teeth grew from her mouth.

Soon the girl was gone.

In her place stood a large gray wolf.

And it knew exactly what it wanted.

Luckily Riley got a dorm room with Wanda, so she didn't have to worry about sharing with one of her mentally damaged classmates.

It was large enough to fit a set of beds, desks, and closets, but they had to share the bathroom down the hall.

Wanda had decorated her side of the room with various photos and trinkets from home.

Riley's side was mostly bare.

All of her possessions had been lost with her van.

Her new clothes were second hand items from Wanda's family. Most of them were either too big or too small.

Wanda sat on her bed scrolling through her phone. Her short pajama pants didn't hide the scratches on her knees.

Tell me more about the guy who knocked into you, Riley wanted to ask, but the words didn't leave her mouth.

That moment felt like a secret between just her and Elijah.

Riley sighed and looked at the textbook on her desk. It described the greatness of werewolves like she was supposed to feel thankful that her whole life had been turned upside down.

The howling of wolves and loud thumping of music from outside their window made it difficult to concentrate.

It was like the whole campus turned into a frat party after dark.

Riley tossed her pencil on the desk.

Was she the only one with homework?

Riley moved across the room to shut the window, only to pull back the curtain to see a guy standing on the grass before the dorm. He was holding an acoustic guitar while staring up at their room.

He was broad with short black hair and large glasses, dressed in a brown leather jacket and ripped jeans.

"Oh, Wanda!" he enthusiastically sang at the top of his lungs. "You make me *wonder* how a girl can be as beautiful as you!"

Riley cringed, resisting the urge to slam the window.

"Wanda," she said. "I think there's some guy out here for you."

"Oh, that's just Jimmy." Wanda didn't look away from her phone. "He did that a lot last year too."

"Wow...that's very......persistent of him."

"Yeah, he's always following me around and bringing me food. Sometimes leaving letters in my locker." She got off the bed and walked over to Riley. "Look at all the cute messages he sent me over the summer."

Wanda pulled up a chat consisting entirely of messages from Jimmy. There were well over a hundred. The most recent ones said

WANDA WHERE ARE YOU!

WHY AREN'T YOU REPLYING TO MY MESSAGES!

I WILL FIND YOU!

I WILL PUT MY OFFSPRING INSIDE YOU! AND WE'LL BE TOGETHER FOREVER!

WANDA!!!!!

"Oh." Riley wasn't sure what to say. "Do you want me to show you how to block him?"

"Block him?"

"I mean, this is pretty serious harassment."

"Nah," said Wanda. "My ex-boyfriend was way worse."

"Oh."

Wanda shifted closer with a devilish smile on her face.

Riley was overcome with a feeling of dread.

"You know....." said Wanda. "Tommy was too shy to say anything at lunch, but he's super into you. You should give him a chance."

For fucks sake, Riley thought.

"And this wouldn't have anything to do with the money he gets for every kid?" Riley asked.

"Nah...well maybe a little, but it could still be a lot of fun."

Riley tried her best to keep a straight face. She owed Wanda a lot, but that didn't extend to screwing her cousin.

"I'm tired," Riley said. "I'm gonna go to bed."

"I've heard that he gives decent oral."

"Goodnight Wanda."

Riley slipped under the sheets of her bed and pulled the blanket up over her head, trying to drown out the sound of Jimmy's terrible singing.

"Sure you wanna go to bed now?" said Wanda. "Now's the best time for hooking up."

"I'll see you tomorrow, Wanda."

"Okay, goodnight," Wanda replied before slipping out of the room.

Riley tossed and turned under the covers, trying to find a comfortable position.

She had already suffered enough for one day, there was no way that the next day could be any worse.

Right?

CHAPTER FOUR

She was running on four legs, bounding past trees and bushes as she dashed through the forest.

The leafy foliage was cool under her paws.

She could hear the chirping of insects, the rustling of small animals, and the cries of other wolves.

She was one with nature.

A beast. A hunter.

It was like her human self never existed.

All that mattered was satisfying the hunger inside her.

And *him.*

He was near.

She could smell his scent on the wind, calling her closer.

The wolf was more than happy to comply.

She emerged into a clearing, surrounded by thick foliage. The dry grass was littered with fallen leaves. The scent of mildew permeated the air.

He was already there.

Before her stood a large white wolf.

His fur was pale like the moon. His sharp teeth gleamed in the darkness. His strong body made her legs weak, and the intoxicating scent radiating off him was enough to drive anyone mad.

Him.

The white wolf shuddered and shook.

Bones broke and realigned themselves. Glimmering fur was replaced with pale skin, taking the shape of a large human man.

Elijah.

His large bulky body towered over Riley, smooth chest heaving up and down with each labored breath.

He was naked, well defined muscles and large upper arms fully on display.

Not to mention his cock.

It stood fully erect between two powerful thighs, swollen and ready to burst.

Elijah looked straight at her, but there was something vacant about his gaze.

He was there, but also not.

Like the animal inside him had taken control.

Riley's body couldn't help but react to his.

She transformed, slowly returning to her human form.

Elijah's breath hitched.

His hungry eyes gazed over her round breasts and tanned skin, pausing at the glimmering fluid smeared to her thigh.

He hadn't even touched her, but she was already dripping.

Elijah moved towards her like a tiger stalking its prey, taking one step in front of the other without looking away.

Do it, Riley's whole body screamed.

Elijah grabbed a hold of Riley's hair and tilted her head back, crushing his mouth against hers.

His lips were quick and brutal, everything that Riley knew that she shouldn't want, but couldn't help but enjoy.

She wrapped her arms around his neck to keep herself upright, parting her lips to allow his tongue inside.

Closer....

She moaned as his large thigh slipped between her legs, rubbing against her soaked entrance.

His pulsing erection pressed against her stomach.

More...

Elijah ripped his mouth away and shoved Riley, tackling her to the forest floor.

She let out a growl and snapped at his hand, but allowed his large body to climb over hers.

Together...

Riley pulled herself to her hands and knees, arse in the air and thighs wide apart.

Elijah slipped his thick cock straight into her wet heat, bottoming out without any resistance.

He let out a low groan as the euphoria hit him.

Forever...

He moved his cock with deep powerful thrusts, groaning every time he was consumed by a strong wave of pleasure.

Riley relished the sensation, crying out when his cock hit the right spot.

There was no gentle love making between them.

They were animals focused solely on screwing each other's brains out.

Before Riley knew it, she was cumming.

Pleasure exploded outwards from her center as her body sucked his thick dick deeper.

Elijah gasped as he climaxed, spraying his seed straight into her fertile womb.

Pleasure.

It was all Riley could feel as her climax approached, threatening to burst forth at any moment.

Just a little more.

It felt so good.

She was almost there.

A blaring alarm startled her awake.

Riley's eyes shot open to see her bedroom, basked in morning light.

Wanda was sitting at her desk, dressed in a yellow T-shirt and short denim skirt. She applied purple eyeshadow while looking at herself in a handheld mirror.

Was it all just a dream?

Riley quickly realized that her hand was down her pajama pants.

Her fingers were soaked, like she'd been masturbating in her sleep.

She quickly ripped her hand away.

"Don't worry," said Wanda with a casual wave of her hand. "It happens to me all the time. Feel free to keep going."

"I..I...I." Riley wanted to cry. She'd never done something so embarrassing. "I'm gonna go have a shower."

She grabbed her clothes off her desk chair and fled down the hall.

Riley didn't want to touch herself.

She was still upset about being seen by Wanda, but her body felt hot and bothered. It was painful to come so close to climax and then leave herself hanging.

Riley reached down to touch her clit, moaning at the sudden relief.

She ended up masturbating under the shower spray.

Riley placed one hand over her mouth to muffle the moans as her fingers worked the space between her legs.

Elijah's naked body was fresh in her mind. She could still feel his hard cock pounding against her insides.

It wasn't the first time that she'd had a sex dream about someone, but it had never been so intense.

She'd never felt such a powerful need to touch herself.

Riley braced herself against the shower wall as her groin went numb. She shuddered as her orgasm consumed her, washing over her body in waves.

It was just a dream, Riley thought as she gasped for breath. *It doesn't mean anything.*

The post orgasm high gave her enough courage to face Wanda again.

They grabbed breakfast, then walked to class together.

"It's not good to hold it in for too long," said Wanda. "Sometimes you need to fuck it out of your system."

"Okay, Wanda," Riley replied, hoping that her friend would quickly drop it.

"What about that guy?" Wanda pointed to a lanky teen who was leaning against the wall smoking a vape. "He's always good for a quick fuck."

"I'll keep that in mind," Riley mumbled.

"Wanda! Riley!" Tommy waved at them from across the hall.

Shit! Riley thought.

She wanted to run, but Wanda was already enthusiastically waving him over.

Tommy bounded across the hall towards them.

"Hey Riley," he said with a giant smile. "You look nice today."

Could he lay it on any thicker? Riley thought.

She was dressed in one of her least sexy outfits, an oversized black T-shirt and a pair of washed out jeans.

"Good morning, Tommy," Riley curtly replied.

"Do you remember where your class is?" asked Tommy. "I can walk you there today if you like."

"That's very nice of you." Riley tried her best to remain polite. "But I think that I can find it on my own."

"Are you sure?" said Tommy. "It's really no-"

He was cut off by someone shoving him as they walked past, causing Tommy to stumble forward.

Tommy swore under his breath as he regained his balance, head snapping around to see who had shoved him.

It was Elijah.

He was dressed in a brand name jacket and jeans, along with expensive sneakers that would have cost Riley a month's wage.

His blonde hair was neatly combed back and his face was freshly shaved, completely different from his wild appearance in Riley's dream.

Seeing him again made her heart race.

Delicious.. was the first thought that popped into her mind.

Elijah was accompanied by his equally blonde haired blue eyed friends.

They were busy talking amongst themselves.

Elijah glared at Tommy coldly.

"Watch where you're going, mix-breed," he said before continuing down the hall.

"Fucking Elijah Brant," Tommy muttered under his breath.

Riley snapped out of her trance. "Elijah Brant?"

"His family are all higher ups," said Tommy. "Makes him think that he can do whatever he wants."

"Oh, I see," said Riley while trying to appear as disinterested as possible.

"See that girl there." Tommy pointed to a girl in their group, a stunning beauty with long pale hair and immaculate skin. "The two of them have been engaged since before they could walk. They'll probably be running this place one day, and there's nothing that we can do about it."

"Oh...that's terrible," Riley murmured while trying to get her racing heart under control.

Her stupid body didn't seem to care that Elijah was already taken.

She fought the urge to rub her thighs together.

Wanda bit her lower lip, looking between Riley and Elijah.

"Come on," Wanda said. "We'll be late."

She took hold of Riley's hand and pulled her away.

Class was still a shit show.

Davis had realized that there were plenty of werewolf women who would happily screw him. He had spent the evening getting friendly with several of them without consulting his girlfriend.

"But you told me that it would be just us from now on," his girlfriend sobbed at her desk.

"I know, babe." Davis softly patted her back. "But I got a duty now. Gotta help make the next generation."

"But you already have five kids," she cried.

Riley cringed and rubbed her temples.

Mr. Bites was still immune to the chaos around him. He spent three hours explaining the werewolf hierarchy, naming old people that Riley was supposed to be subservient to from now on.

"And then the Elders take orders from the Grand Elders," said Mr. Bites while drawing diagrams on the blackboard. "Who then take orders from the Grand High Elders, who then takes orders from the Highest Elder."

Riley tuned out and started counting the cracks in the wall.

She was thrilled when class finally broke for lunch. As screwed up as the school was, at least the food was good.

Riley made her way through the sea of students towards the cafeteria, dodging a large group of wolves that came sprinting down the hall.

She entered the large room and grabbed a tray of food, only to see Tommy walking towards her.

He'd changed into a clean shirt and his long hair was neatly tied back. He strolled towards her with a confident swagger that made Riley cringe.

"Hey Riley," he greeted with a large toothy smile. "We saved you a seat."

"Oh," Riley nervously laughed. "How thoughtful of you."

"No problem. We always take good care of our own."

Riley nodded and followed behind him. It was difficult to tell if he was hitting on her, or just being friendly.

"So how are you liking the school?" Tommy asked.

"It's very....different."

"Yeah, I thought you'd say that. My dad was an outsider too. He said that he found it weird at first, but he eventually got used to it."

"Oh....how's he doing now?"

"Weird as always, but he found the right group. In werewolf society, who you hang out with is super important."

They reached a table full of older students.

"These are some of my friends," said Tommy. "Trent, Betty, Xavier, Alexander, Lucifer, Maximillion, and Fred."

Riley tried her best to nod and greet everyone, but it was difficult with Wanda making out with a guy halfway down the table.

Wanda was shamelessly straddling his lap, moving her lips against his like the world was about to end.

"Hey Riley," said Wanda while grinding down on the guy's groin. "You remember Jimmy, right? The two of you met last night."

"Hey," Jimmy groaned, but turned his attention straight back to Wanda. "Yeah, that's great, Wanda baby."

You have to be joking? Riley thought while remembering the creepy messages that Wanda showed her the night before.

The guy was dripping in red flags, but Wanda didn't seem to care.

Riley took a seat next to Tommy. She attempted to eat her food, but Wanda's loud moaning along with Tommy's awkward come ons, made it impossible to relax.

"So Riley." Tommy's hand twitched like he was thinking of wrapping it around her shoulder. "What's your favorite position? Did my cousin tell you that I like to do it doggy style?"

Riley's fork slipped from her grip, clattering against the table.

"Geez man," said one of Tommy's friends. "Do you think you could lay it on any thicker?"

"Girls love honesty." Tommy winked. "Don't you, Riley?"

Riley paused to swallow her food. "Well...If I ever break my self imposed celibacy rule, I'll let you know."

"See guys," Tommy laughed. "She does dig me."

"Save it for Catlyn," said his friend. "Or Joanna, or the other dozen girls you already hit on this morning."

"*Shhhh,*" Tommy hissed. "What have I told you about messing with my game?"

A laugh escaped Riley's mouth.

She finally found herself starting to relax, but then Jimmy pulled up Wanda's skirt to expose her naked rear.

Jimmy pulled his hand back and gave Wanda's arse a hard slap.

Wanda let out a cry of surprise.

"Yeah, you like that, don't you?" Jimmy growled. He pulled down the zipper on his jeans to free his bulging cock. "Are you gonna be a good girl and let daddy stick it in you?"

Riley jumped to her feet. "I think I'm gonna go study... in the library."

"But this school doesn't have a library," said Tommy.

"Well..." Riley tried not to look at Wanda sliding down onto Jimmy's dick. "I...better go talk to them about starting one."

She spun on her heels and dashed out of the cafeteria before any one could stop her.

Riley wanted to go somewhere quiet without people humping each other, but they were everywhere.

Pairs of young adults were screwing in the hallways and empty class-rooms like their lunch was laced with Viagra.

There was one girl who looked to be nine months pregnant, bracing herself against the wall as she was being drilled into from behind.

"Are you sure that this will make the baby come faster," she gasped.

"Trust me," the guy huffed while thrusting his hips. "They don't call me the labor inducer for nothing."

Riley pushed open a side door leading out to the back of the school. She followed the wall around until she found a neglected rose garden.

There was a small courtyard overgrown with weeds, and a pile of worn desks that looked like they'd been sitting there for years.

Riley sat down on a short brick wall to catch her breath.

It was all too much.

As soon as she thought she could handle this place, another curve ball was thrown in her direction.

She didn't belong with these people.

How long would it take before they realized that and cast her out?

The *ping* of a phone notification reached her ears.

Riley snapped her head around to the other side of the courtyard, searching for the source of the sound.

It was *him.*

Elijah stood there looking straight at her, lower lip twitching like he was unsure of what to say.

Riley froze.

Fuck, she thought.

Illicit thoughts about his dick immediately swarmed her head.

"What are you doing here?" she blurted out.

"Me?" Elijah said. "I could ask you the same thing."

"I don't have to explain myself to you," Riley snapped back.

Crap, she thought, trying to stop the heat rising to her face. *Why does he have to be so hot?*

"The weather is nice." Elijah averted his gaze like he was too embarrassed to look at her. "So I just wanted to be outside."

"Yeah, me too," Riley said, even though it was a lie.

"Oh."

"Yeah."

"That's cool."

"Yeah..."

Silence dragged on between them.

"I saw you with that group of half-breeds." Elijah nervously tugged on his shirt sleeve. "You should ditch them. They're no good for you."

"And how would you know what's good for me?" she snapped.

Elijah bit his lower lip.

Just the sight caused an uncomfortable pulsing in Riley's groin.

I think you already know, his gaze said.

"I should go." Riley pulled herself to her feet, determined to flee the situation before it got any weirder. "En....Enjoy your roses."

"Hey wait!" Elijah called out after her, but she didn't stop.

Riley forced herself to walk away before she did something that she'd regret.

CHAPTER FIVE

That night Riley was a wolf.

She bounded through the forest with ease, following an invisible pull that urged her forward.

Come....

She emerged into a large clearing full of other wolves. They shed their animal forms to become human, naked from head to toe.

*Come dance with us...*they sang without saying a word.

The beating of drums echoed throughout the forest.

There was a large bonfire in the middle of the clearing. Young men and women danced in a circle.

Wanda was there, along with Jimmy and his friends, fresh cum running down her naked thighs.

Wanda stumbled towards Riley, struggling to remain standing.

"Here, drink this," laughed Wanda. She held out a glass bottle filled with a clear liquid. "It will make you feel good."

Riley shivered and returned to her human form. She took the bottle from Wanda's hand, taking a large sip.

The strong liquid burned her throat.

"Great isn't it?" Jimmy wrapped an arm around Wanda from behind. He pressed her forward then slid his thick cock straight into her wet entrance, letting out a hiss. "Really heightens the sensation."

He pounded into Wanda's willing body like nobody was watching, spreading her legs apart to plunge in as deep as possible.

"Yeah, baby," Jimmy moaned. "Come on daddy's dick. I'll give you a big litter this spring."

Wanda cried out with every strong thrust.

But it wasn't just them.

All around her people were fucking.

The light of the fire illuminated their sweaty bodies as they mercilessly used each other.

Come... be with us...

Riley shuddered and took a step back.

No.

There was somewhere else that she needed to be.

She slipped back into the shadows, stumbling over rocks and tree branches as she moved away from the circle.

He was near.

She could smell his scent on the wind, rich and addictive.

Come to me...

Riley kept walking forward, the space between her legs growing wetter with each taste of his sweet aroma.

Let's be together....

Large hands took hold of her shoulders, shoving Riley forward against a tree. Warm lips attacked her neck, causing Riley to arch back into the sensation.

It was *him.*

Elijah's firm chest pressed against her back as his large fingers crept between her legs, testing her wet warmth before slipping inside. His fingers slowly moved in and out, rubbing against her clit with each slide.

Riley placed both hands against the cool tree bark to brace herself, moaning as electric pleasure built in her lower body.

One of his hands cupped her breast, gently squeezing as his teeth nipped her ear.

Riley cried out.

Her whole body trembled as the sensations became overwhelming.

Elijah urged her thighs further apart.

He rubbed his rock hard cock against her soft arse, then slipped it between her legs, sliding back and forth through her fluids while tightly gripping her thighs.

Riley shuddered every time that it rubbed her clit.

His cock caught on her entrance, then plunged inside, pressing against her cervix.

Riley hissed as he began to thrust, pounding against her body with no control over himself.

Her eyes screwed shut as she cried out with each powerful wave of pleasure, fully giving herself over to the sensation.

Yes. This was right.

This was where she was supposed to be.

They would breed again and again until her stomach was swollen with his offspring. She'd give birth to them all, then they'd start again the following year.

There was no need to think.

Just fuck again and again like her werewolf body wanted.

The inner animal refused to be suppressed by trivial human emotions.

Elijah picked up speed as his climax approached, groaning as he came deep inside her.

Riley jolted awake.

She was sitting on the shower floor, slumped up against the wall with her face pressed against the cold tiles.

She was naked from head to toe, soaked hair plastered to her neck and shoulders.

The hot water had turned cold, stinging her skin.

The last thing she remembered was going to bed.

A fluorescent light flickered above her head. The room was bright enough to tell that it was morning.

What the fuck.

It was happening again.

Riley had plenty of blackouts since becoming a werewolf, but it had been weeks since her last episode.

Wanda's father said that it was her mind adjusting. The human and wolf were fighting each other.

It made it difficult to differentiate what memories were real and which were just crazed delusions.

But one thing was obvious.

Her inner wolf wanted to fuck Elijah Brant.

Out of all the men on campus, she had no idea why her stupid wolf brain decided to focus on that one.

Sure he was hot, but given what she knew about him, he was clearly an arsehole. She wouldn't have spared him a second if they met on the outside.

And the sex.

Riley was never into rough or violent sex, but her inner wolf seemed to love it. It wanted to be pinned to the ground and pumped full of cum like there was no tomorrow.

What sort of fucked up being had she become?

Riley pulled herself to her feet, limping as her leg cramped up.

There was no towel or clothing in sight, so she wrapped her naked body in the shower curtain.

Riley returned to her room to see Wanda watching videos on her phone.

Wanda was already dressed for the day. She looked too well put together to have been part of a drunk werewolf orgie the night before.

"Hey," said Wanda as her fingers flew across the phone screen. "I was wondering when you'd show up."

Riley knew that all she had to do was ask Wanda if the previous night was real, but she was afraid.

What if it had really happened? What if she really had been out screwing some arsehole after dark?

If she didn't ask, then it was easier to pretend that it was only a dream.

Riley opened her closet, reaching for a T-shirt and jeans. "I just got held up, that's all."

Wanda let out a low whistle.

"What's that supposed to mean?" Riley said.

"Nothing. Unless you want it to."

Riley slipped on her clothes, then ran her fingers through her long hair to work out the knots.

"I just....." Riley paused as she searched for the right words. "Sometimes don't feel like myself."

"If it's about your new inner wolf, my only advice is the same as before."

"Which was?"

"Don't fight it."

"Yeah..but..that's easy for you. You were born a werewolf."

"But it doesn't matter that much."

Riley let out a sigh of frustration.

Wanda's human and wolf selves had been in balance since she was born. No way could she understand what Riley was going through.

Wanda didn't seem to understand the terror of losing control of yourself.

"Yeah, you're probably right," Riley muttered, gathering her textbooks and placing them in her bag. "Let's just get to class."

Riley spent the morning convincing herself that being screwed by Elijah was just a weird sex dream.

She told herself that Wanda was wrong.

She didn't need to give into any creepy urges.

She'd tell her weird arse inner wolf who was in control and retake her life.

The first step was mastering her stupid class.

That morning, Mr. Bites had them all assemble in the woods.

Davis and his girlfriend were gone, like they'd both worked out that attendance didn't matter.

Half the class were also missing, but their teacher didn't care.

"This morning we'll be doing some mentoring," Mr. Bites said brightly. "So I've invited some older students to pair up with you."

There was a collective groan amongst her classmates.

They stood around waiting as the older students gradually showed up. Several of them looked like they'd been blackmailed into being there.

To Riley's relief, she was paired with a friendly looking girl with long red curly hair. She wore a large white summer dress with a brown leather belt.

"Just to let you know," the girl said brightly. "I'm not like *some* people here. I totally support your kind integrating into our community."

"Thanks..." said Riley. "I think."

The girl held out her hand for Riley to shake. "I'm Heather. I-"

Heather was suddenly shoved out of the way by a slim blonde girl. She was well dressed with immaculate pale skin.

She angrily glared at Riley without saying a word.

"Latavia," said their teacher. "Why don't you come work with-"

The girl snapped her head around to glare at Mr. Bites, letting out a low growl.

"Or not," he said and hurried away.

Shit, Riley thought. *It's the fiancé.*

Latavia turned her attention back to Riley. "Stay away from Elijah," she spat.

Riley couldn't help but laugh.

It seemed hilarious that this beautiful girl who looked like a doll, could in any way feel threatened by her.

"Don't worry," said Riley. "As if I'd ever be interested."

"Do you think I'm stupid," said Latavia. "I know that you're trying to dig your grubby little claws into him."

"There must be some mis-"

"Ugly, and a liar," Latavia huffed. "I guess it's true that all munchers are trash."

Riley was taken back. "Muncher?"

"You're only a werewolf because some crazy stray munched on you, so that makes you a muncher."

"O...kay," said Riley. She would have felt insulted if it didn't sound so ridiculous.

"They should have just left you alone to live in the wild," said Latavia. "Your kind doesn't belong in this place."

Screw you.. You fucking bitch, Riley wanted to snap, but she held back.

Perhaps all the inbreeding had made Latavia insane.

"Don't worry," said Riley. "I don't plan on staying in this dump for long."

"Good!" Latavia spat. "Because Elijah and I are engaged." She shoved a hand out before Riley, flashing a large gold ring. "We're getting married next year and I'm not gonna let some stupid muncher ruin it."

"Whatever," Riley muttered. "Good luck with that."

"Don't you dare come near him again."

"Okay."

"Good."

"Good."

With an arrogant huff, Latavia huffed and spun on her feet, disappearing into the woods.

"Latavia!" Mr. Bites called out after her. "Don't you want that extra credit?"

Latavia didn't return.

Riley crossed her arms, suppressing the urge to punch something.

If Latavia wanted Elijah so badly, then she was more than welcome to him.

CHAPTER SIX

Things got better after Latavia stormed off.

Riley's first partner returned and they spent the day exploring the woods together.

Heather showed Riley edible berries and plants.

She seemed sweet enough, but ignorant about how the human world worked.

"I can't imagine what it would be like not to hunt your own food," said Heather. "How do humans even survive?"

"It's not that hard," said Riley. "We usually just go to a supermarket?"

"Supermarket?"

"You know, a supermarket."

Heather looked perplexed.

"Seriously?" said Riley. "You don't know what a supermarket is?"

"No." Heather shook her head. "My clan lives in the mountains away from the humans. My father said that it's better that way. He says that humans are all primitive barbarians who can't understand our greatness."

"Oh." Riley had no idea how to reply.

"No offense," Heather added. "At least you're one of us now, so you don't have to worry about their backwardness anymore."

"Wow, lucky me," Riley nervously laughed.

Riley was exhausted that evening when she returned to her room.

She was looking forward to taking a hot shower and relaxing in bed, but she opened the door to find Wanda and Jimmy going at it on top of Wanda's sheets.

They were both fully naked.

Jimmy was lying back on the bed as Wanda rode his cock, rocking back and forth as she let out small cries.

"Yeah, baby," Jimmy groaned. "Cum for daddy."

"Oh, hey Riley," Wanda said with a smile while grinding down on his cock. "Don't mind us."

"Yeah." Jimmy pumped up into Wanda's wet heat. "Just pretend that we're not here."

"I....I." Riley averted her gaze, but the image of them fucking was firmly burnt into her brain. "I think that I'll just come back later."

Riley quickly shut the door and dashed down the hall.

Where was she supposed to go?

The school building was off limits after dark, so Riley wandered the halls of the dorm until she came to the common room.

There was an air hockey table, a T.V, and several shelves of board games and books.

She spotted Heather in front of the T.V, curled up on the sofa while immersed in a tacky game show.

Riley thought of going over to say hello, when a familiar laugh made her insides freeze.

Elijah was sitting at a nearby table with his friends. They were playing poker while passing a bottle of vodka between them.

Latavia had one arm wrapped around his shoulder, laughing as she watched his cards. Her immaculate nails tapped his hard bicep.

Riley backed away. She didn't have the mental energy to face him or his shitty girlfriend.

She walked out the main entrance and into the night. The howling of wolves echoed from deep within the forest.

Riley walked through the trees until she found a large rock. She took a seat, wrapping her arms around herself to ward off the cold.

Wanda and Jimmy couldn't keep fucking forever. All she had to do was wait for them to leave or pass out.

"You seem to like being alone," said a deep voice from behind her.

Riley jumped.

She quickly turned to see Elijah, dressed casually in a pair of worn jeans and a hoodie. His hair poked out at odd angles and his pale cheeks appeared flushed from the vodka.

Shit, she thought. *What is he doing here?"*

As shocked as she was to see him, part of her was glad.

He was all alone and smelled delicious, but that only made her more afraid.

Riley eyed the path behind him, looking for a way to escape.

Elijah could see what she was thinking. "No, wait. I just want to-"

In a split second, Riley was on her feet. She dashed into the thick forest before her.

She needed to get away.

Elijah's footsteps echoed behind her. "Hey! Wait!"

Riley didn't stop.

She ran through the foliage while fighting the urge to transform. She knew that she was faster in wolf form, but she didn't trust her animal body.

Just the sight of him was enough to make her wet.

With a low growl, Elijah lunged at her, knocking Riley to the ground. He tried to pin her down, but Riley kicked him away, scrambling back to her feet.

"Why are you running?" he cried.

"Stay away from me!"

"Why?" he said, hurt evident in his voice.

"I think that you know why!"

Elijah looked taken back like she'd slapped him in the face, but then his mouth twisted into an angry scowl.

"I don't know how things work between humans," he said. "But *real* werewolves don't sleep with each other and then pretend that nothing happened."

Riley's breath hitched as her mind went blank.

So it was real. They did have sex the previous night.

"That.." Riley stuttered. "That's because…"

She had no idea how to deal with this. Mr. Bites never taught them about werewolf fuckbuddies.

Silence dragged on between them.

"Forget it," Elijah muttered and turned to leave. "I know when I'm not wanted."

No, don't go! Riley wanted to scream, but she couldn't get the words out. She silently watched him walk away.

It felt like someone was stabbing a knife through her heart.

"Fuck," Riley swore and kicked a tree, hissing in agony when pain shot up her leg.

What the hell was wrong with her?

Riley didn't have the courage to return to the dorms. She walked deeper into the forest until she found a small cave, resting against the rock wall.

She found it oddly soothing. The cool night air and the faint chirping of insects lured her to sleep.

The wolf wasn't like Riley.

It knew what it wanted and how to take it.

She gracefully moved through the night like a specter, silently stalking her prey.

A small black rabbit bounced through the leafy foliage before her, unaware of its impending doom.

It was time to eat.

The wolf pounced on the rabbit and dove its teeth into the animal's warm neck, biting down until it stopped struggling.

Blood filled the wolf's mouth as it ripped the meat from the bones with sickening cracks, devouring it in a frenzy.

It tasted rich and delicious, but it wasn't enough to fill the gnawing hunger inside.

It was time to hunt something else.

Riley shifted back to her human form.

She wiped the blood from her mouth with the back of her hand, smearing it across her face.

Foliage crushed under her bare feet as she moved to her next target.

You're mine....

She emerged into a clearing to find Elijah sitting in the center, sadly looking up at the full moon.

"What do you want?" he sighed.

You... the wolf sang.

Elijah turned to Riley, breath hitching. His blue eyes drank in her naked form.

Her soft skin appeared paler in the moonlight. Blood smeared her face and chest.

She held his gaze without flinching.

You can run if you want, but I will always find you...

Elijah nervously swallowed.

Riley gracefully moved towards him.

She took hold of his shoulders and pushed him back to the ground.

Elijah crumbled beneath her touch.

She pinned him down and pressed her lips to his warm neck, sucking the skin as her naked cunt humped his clothed groin.

Elijah gasped, writhing beneath her.

"*Fuck,*" he hissed as a wave of pleasure hit him. "Are you for real?"

Riley only growled in response.

She tugged at his shirt and pants, quickly pulling them off with Elijah's help.

Her body moved against his, dripping pussy running over his swollen dick.

Elijah hissed and gripped her thighs to hold on, watching her full breasts bounce above him.

Riley slid down onto his thick cock, bringing it deep inside until their groins were flush against each other.

She ground her clit against his pelvic bone, chasing the all-consuming high.

"You like my big cock, huh?" Elijah gasped, thrusting his hips up into her wet heat. "Just take it... take as much as you want."

Riley didn't need his permission.

She moved her hips as pleasure began to build in her core. So large and consuming that it was impossible to stop.

She raked her nails against his hard chest, watching as he shuddered and moaned beneath her.

She didn't expect him to take it so obediently.

He was her bitch now.

Riley closed her eyes and allowed the sensations to guide her, leading her to a wonderful climax.

Pure joy overtook her lower body before she suddenly crashed, frantically thrusting as her pussy clenched and sucked him deeper.

Her orgasm was enough to push Elijah over the edge. He quickly pumped his hips as cum sprayed from his cock.

She'd take it all.

Elijah's body was large and strong. She'd milk him for all he was worth to give her healthy offspring. Her children would become the dominant ones in the pack.

The wolf inside her refused to settle for anything less.

CHAPTER SEVEN

Riley jolted awake.

She was shocked to see an unfamiliar ceiling above her head.

This wasn't her bed.

Shit.

Riley could feel warm naked skin pressed against hers.

She looked to her right to see Elijah's peaceful sleeping face beside her.

Her naked body was tangled with his. The space between her legs was soaked and she could feel his seed on her thighs.

This time she couldn't pass it off as a dream.

There was no denying that they'd slept together.

It was all too much for Riley's fragile mind to handle.

She had to get away.

She attempted to slip out from underneath the sheets, but Elijah's grip tightened around her waist, pulling her closer.

He nuzzled his face against her neck, inhaling her scent with a sigh.

"Where do you think you're going?" His deep voice reverberated against her skin.

All thoughts of running flew out the window as Elijah's wet lips pressed against Riley's neck, stoking a fire in her core.

He slowly licked her skin as Riley squirmed in his grasp, shifting herself closer in search of more contact.

She was wet and ready for him.

Elijah slipped a large hand between her legs, running his fingers over her soaked pussy. "You want this, don't you?"

He paused when Riley didn't answer.

Riley panicked. She bucked her hips into his touch.

"Yeah," she moaned.

Elijah pressed kisses to her cheek while running his fingers back and forth along her entrance and clit, spreading warm fluid over her most sensitive areas, immersing her lower half in intoxicating sensations.

Riley gasped and arched her back. She spread her legs wider as her hips rolled into his touch.

Elijah continued rubbing, watching her moan and gasp beside him. He rubbed his growing erection against her soft thigh.

Riley wrapped her arms around his neck to hold on as her climax approached, consuming her whole being like a supernova.

Overwhelming joy washed over her until she suddenly crashed, gasping and panting for breath as Elijah rubbed her through the orgasm.

She pushed his hand away when it became too much.

Her whole body felt warm and sedated. She welcomed his eager lips against her own.

It felt right.

Elijah rolled on top of her, slipping his hard cock straight inside her wet entrance, bottoming out with one thrust.

"You feel it too, don't you?" he said softly, rolling his hips. "This connection between us."

"Yeah," Riley whispered.

He gripped her hand, weaving his fingers through hers as his cock slowly thrust in and out. "Can't you see? We're fated to be together."

Riley nodded. It sounded insane, but she would have agreed to anything at that moment.

"You feel so good," Elijah hissed. "So wet and soft. Sex has never felt like this for me before."

"Yeah." Riley's breath hitched. "Me neither."

She'd done plenty of awkward fumbling with her ex-boyfriend, but it was never as intense as this.

His cock felt sublime against her insides. She was incomplete without him buried deep inside her.

"*Fuck,*" he hissed, picking up the pace. "I'm gonna cum. I'm gonna cum inside you."

No, don't, Riley wanted to say, but for some reason she just didn't care. She wanted him.

She wanted to see his face contort in ecstasy as he pumped his seed deep inside her.

Screw the consequences.

Elijah thrust hard and fast until he came with a moan, spraying his fluids deep into her womb.

Riley watched his powerful body move back and forth, filling her with every rock of his hips.

He was beautiful.

Elijah collapsed against her once he was through, holding her close and rubbing soft circles against her upper arm.

"Wow," he murmured, resting his face against her neck. "That was...wow."

Riley shifted beneath him. Watching him cum inside her had made her horny again.

She wanted to pin him to the bed and press her aching clit to his lips, rubbing against his tongue until she came on his face.

Why not spend the whole day in bed playing with each other?

"Can you keep it down next time," moaned a male voice from the other side of the room. "Some of us are still trying to sleep."

Riley quickly turned towards the voice to see Elijah's roommate lying back on his bed.

The guy pulled a thick blanket over his head. Only his blonde hair was poking out.

Heat rushed to Riley's face.

He had seen and heard everything.

What if he told everyone?

Riley jumped out of bed, dragging the white bed sheet with her.

"No wait!" Elijah called out.

His hand dashed out to grab her, but it got nothing but air.

Luckily naked people wandering the halls was nothing new in the strange fuck fest Riley lived in.

She walked past a naked guy screwing his girlfriend next to an open door, like there wasn't a perfectly fine bed a few feet away.

Wanda wasn't in their room.

She and Jimmy were probably busy role-playing his strange daddy fantasies.

Riley showered and got dressed for the day, removing all traces of Elijah from her skin.

When she looked at herself in the mirror, she could almost see a normal person staring back.

Was this the way things were going to be from now on? Would her body sleepwalk out to have unprotected sex every night?

Get it together, she told herself, splashing cold water on her face. *You're better than this.*

Riley found Wanda at breakfast.

Her friend looked thoroughly fucked. There were hickies down her neck and bruises on her wrists. She was wearing yesterday's clothes and her hair was tied back into a messy bun.

Maybe I don't look any different? Riley thought to herself, adjusting her collar to cover the lower half of her neck.

Riley grabbed a tray of food and walked over to her friend.

"Hey you," Wanda said with a large grin. "Did you have fun last night?"

Riley flinched.

"Just the usual," she mumbled and slid into a seat opposite Wanda.

"Come on," Wanda whispered and leaned in closer. "I want to hear all the juicy details. Who did you sleep with?"

Riley took a bite of her eggs. "Can we talk about it later?"

She looked over Wanda's shoulder to see Elijah sitting at a different table with his friends.

He took one look at Riley, but then quickly turned away.

At least he was sensible enough not to broadcast their strange relationship to the world.

Wanda turned to follow Riley's line of sight.

"Oh," Wanda said. "Don't tell me that it was one of them?"

Riley looked down at her food. "Can we please just drop it?"

"Was it Augustus Hunt? I heard that he has a big cock, but he's known for leaving bruises."

Riley shook her head.

"Damien Alice?"

"No."

"Patrick Moon?"

"No."

"Elijah Brant?"

Riley froze.

"Oh, Riley," Wanda sighed, disappointment evident in her voice. "Why did it have to be that guy?"

"What do you mean *that guy*?" Riley's suppressed anger slowly bubbled to the surface. "I'm not the one screwing a walking red flag."

"What's that supposed to mean?"

"Jimmy is clearly a creepy stalker, but you have no problem letting him into your pants."

"This isn't about me. Elijah Brant is-"

"You're such a hypocrite," Riley snapped, slamming her fork on the table. "You expect me to be okay with your weird life choices, but then you judge me."

"Riley. I just-"

"I can't take this right now." Riley picked up her tray and got to her feet. "Why don't you just go screw Jimmy or something."

Riley didn't stay to see Wanda's reaction. She returned her tray then walked out the cafeteria.

Riley thought of going straight back to her room and climbing back under the covers, until she remembered that Wanda would be there later.

Riley paused in the hallway, leaning against the wall to catch her breath.

Guilt clawed at her stomach.

She said too much.

Sure Wanda was strange and Riley didn't like Jimmy, but she shouldn't have snapped back at her friend.

Wanda was only looking out for Riley, even if her concern was unwelcome.

Riley was thinking about going back to apologize, when two strong arms wrapped around her waist.

A warm body pressed against her back, as a familiar scent filled her nostrils.

"Found you," Elijah whispered.

His teeth bit down on her earlobe.

Riley shuddered, adrenaline and excitement pumping through her veins.

His touch was like a drug.

"I've been thinking." Elijah rubbed his growing erection against her soft behind. "About how you felt wrapped around my cock."

"Really?" Riley subconsciously relaxed into his touch.

Elijah pressed soft kisses against her neck, basking in Riley's reaction.

"So soft and warm." His fingers crept up Riley's skirt to grip her naked thigh. "Like paradise."

Riley gasped.

His fingers slipped under her underwear to press against her slit, working their way up further to touch her clit.

She jolted.

"Not here," Riley hissed, squirming against his touch.

"Why not," Elijah said.

He rubbed his fingers back and forth along her apex. His hard cock continued to thrust against her behind.

Riley shuddered. "There...are people here."

"And?"

"It's embarrassing."

Elijah chuckled. "What's there to be embarrassed about?"

"You know," Riley gasped as Elijah hit a particularly sensitive spot.

Elijah took hold of the back of her head, turning her to face a couple who were openly screwing at the end of the hall.

The girl's shirt and bra lay on the floor. Her tits bounced up and down as the guy drilled into her from behind.

"Look at them," Elijah murmured, licking Riley's earlobe. "Nobody cares that they're enjoying each other."

"But-"

"There's no need to hide." He pulled her body closer. "We're only doing what's natural."

Riley nodded, looking towards the wall to try and hide her face.

It was true. Everybody was just going about their day without paying them any attention.

Part of her wanted to try it.

She wanted to openly fuck wherever she wanted.

Elijah tugged at her underwear, pulling it down her thighs until it dropped to the ground. He unzipped his pants to free his swollen erection, running it through her wet folds until it slipped into her warm heat.

Riley shuddered and braced herself against the wall.

Elijah slowly slid his dick back and forth. His hand continued to work her clit, leaving Riley boneless and desperate for more.

"I want to take you to class," he huffed. "And screw you on my lap while the fucking teacher rants on about ethics."

Riley's pussy fluttered around his cock as strong waves of pleasure consumed her.

Elijah let out a moan. "A nice warm orgasm would make everything perfect."

Riley struggled to remain standing as her groin went numb. She didn't care if she was crying or shaking. All that mattered was reaching the end.

Overwhelming pleasure washed over her as the climax hit, immersing her body in joy.

Her pussy clamped around his cock, sucking it deeper as Elijah also let go, spraying his essence deep inside her.

"*Fuck,*" Elijah hissed while frantically pounding. "So good."

He emptied himself out in several fast strokes, burying his cock in all the way.

He held her flush against him, nuzzling his face against her neck.

"Don't you see," he whispered. "The two of us could be so good together."

"Yeah," Riley said, but it may have been the post orgasm high talking.

She felt warm and content. She would have done anything that he wanted at that moment.

Elijah kissed her neck before pulling away.

A trail of cum ran down her thighs after he pulled his cock out.

For once in her life, Riley didn't care. It felt good to openly display the evidence of their joy.

Elijah tucked his dick back in his pants.

He took hold of Riley's hand, pulling her down the hall. "Come with me."

Elijah's classes were on the other side of the school.

Riley pulled her hoodie up over her head, trying to shield her face from the older students.

Class had already started.

A stern elderly woman lectured in front of the chalkboard while thirty students halfheartedly watched.

A few looked asleep, and there was already a couple openly screwing in the corner.

Elijah led her to a desk at the back of the room. He sat down, pulling Riley onto his lap so that she was facing him instead of the board.

"We may be more advanced than our human neighbors," said the teacher. "But we lack their numbers. No true progress can come until-"

Riley turned to watch the teacher, but Elijah took hold of her jaw, facing Riley back towards him.

He crushed his mouth against hers, slowly consuming her lips while running his large fingers through her hair.

Elijah's tongue brushed past Riley's lips to plunder her mouth, sending shockwaves of pleasure straight down to her groin.

"All eyes on me," Elijah whispered before diving in for another kiss.

Riley groaned against his mouth, all sane thoughts leaving her mind.

She rocked against his clothed groin, trying to ease the clawing need between her own legs.

Do it, she wanted to scream. *Put it inside me.*

Elijah took hold of her shoulders to gently push Riley back.

He unzipped his pants, adjusting himself to free his bulging cock, exposing himself to the room.

Nobody stopped him.

Riley licked her lips as excitement pulsed through her veins.

Elijah relaxed back in his chair, signaling Riley to take what she wanted.

Riley pulled up her skirt to rub her soaked pussy against his hard dick, shuddering with pleasure as a smile crept across her face.

Shit. It felt good.

She sank down on his swollen erection, wet pussy still soaked with cum.

Elijah bit his lower lip to stop himself from crying out.

He shuddered as pleasure washed over him.

He slowly rolled his hips to get more friction, gripping Riley's thighs to help her move back and forth.

"Yeah, that's good," he whispered. "Nice and slow."

Elijah kept his eyes to the front of the room while Riley slowly rocked on his cock.

She could see him trying to restrain himself. He kept the pace nice and slow to savor the sensations.

Riley buried her face against his shoulder to muffle her moans.

Something was building.

She slowly ground down on his dick, chasing her own pleasure while trying to draw it out.

Her pussy sucked and contracted around him every time that a strong wave of pleasure hit, causing Riley to pause to catch her breath.

Elijah shuddered and gripped her closer, softly thrusting up into her damp heat.

"It's okay," he hushed. "Don't hold back."

Riley nodded and let go, quickly rocking against him as she chased her climax.

Her groin went numb as she reached the plateau, mind whiting out as pleasure exploded from her center.

She moved against him like a woman possessed, working out the rest of her orgasm on his cock.

So good...

Elijah quietly swore under his breath.

He picked Riley up by her thighs and pushed her onto the desk before them.

He spread her legs wide, then plunged his cock back inside, frantically thrusting like he wanted to own her.

So strong and powerful, Riley thought.

He came without warning, pumping his cum as deep as it could go.

When she thought he was finished, he just kept going, filling her up with his seed.

Mine, Riley thought, relishing in the sensation. *All of it is mine.*

CHAPTER EIGHT

"I...I don't know," Riley huffed as Elijah drilled into her from behind.

Her hands clutched the bed sheets as her pussy fluttered around his dick.

After class, Elijah said that he was tired so they returned to his room.

He soon buried his face between her breasts, sucking on her nipples before turning Riley over to do it doggy style.

It didn't seem normal to screw so much in one day, but Riley couldn't bring herself to leave.

She felt like the spell they were under would end as soon as they were apart.

"You should come out tonight," Elijah said with a slow thrust of his hips. "It will just be some of my friends."

"But Latavia.."

"Don't worry about Latavia. I'll handle her."

Elijah sped up the pace before coming inside her with a moan.

"Yeah," he groaned. "No one feels as good as you."

Riley showered and put on fresh clothes before leaving that evening.

She didn't have the courage to return to her room, so Elijah lent her a hoodie and sweatpants.

They were far too large but Riley didn't care. She enjoyed the feeling of his warm scent against her skin.

Home... her inner wolf sang.

Elijah took hold of her hand and led her into the forest.

"Don't worry," said Elijah like he could sense Riley's unease. "I'll show them all that you're my girl now."

She squeezed his hand.

They emerged into a clearing with a campfire in the middle. There was a picnic blanket covered in snacks and a small speaker blaring hip-hop music.

Several of Elijah's blonde friends were already there, along with a few girls that Riley didn't know.

Latavia didn't waste a second confronting them.

She stormed towards them as though gliding on air, perfectly manicured hands angrily shoved on her hips.

"Why did you bring her here?" Latavia snapped, angrily jabbing a finger at Riley.

Elijah didn't back down.

His grip tightened around Riley's hand. "Last time I checked, you don't own me."

Latavia ground her teeth with frustration.

"Fine," she snapped, throwing her hands in the air. "But if you're going to screw this *thing*, then I'm fucking Patrick."

"Fine," said Elijah. "Be my guest."

"Fine!" Latavia spun on her heels and walked back to the group.

"See," Elijah whispered in Riley's ear. "All worked out."

Riley nodded as relief washed over her.

That was a lot easier than she expected.

Latavia walked straight to a large pale guy. He looked so similar to Elijah that they could have been cousins. She plonked herself down on his lap, grabbed his collar, then furiously made out with him.

Elijah rolled his eyes. "Always the drama queen."

Riley let out a laugh.

She spotted Heather sitting on the lap of another guy.

Heather waved Riley and Elijah over with a giant smile.

"Riley," she laughed. "Fancy meeting you here. Have you met Damien?" She indicated to the guy behind her. "He says that he's going to screw me so hard that I won't be able to walk for a week."

"Wow.." Riley said, searching for the right thing to say. "That's really... .something."

"Right." Heather grinned like she was entirely serious. "I'm sure that father would approve. He's always been telling me that I should reproduce with a purebred."

"Don't worry, babe." Damien slid a large hand up Heather's skirt. "I'm gonna fill you up real good. You'll have the best babies once spring rolls round."

"See," Heather said. "Isn't he great?"

"Yeah," Riley awkwardly laughed. "A real keeper."

Damien passed Elijah a white bottle. "Here man, you should take a drink."

Elijah took a large swig before passing it to Riley.

She took a sip. The taste of coconut and rum burned her tongue.

"So man." Damien patted Elijah on the shoulder. "Is it true what they say? Do muncher girls really bend over backwards for wolf cock?"

Riley almost choked on a mouthful of alcohol.

He couldn't be serious?

Elijah brushed Damien's hand away. "Not today, man."

"But you're the one who-"

Elijah cut him off. "Let's just get wasted and have a good time."

"Okay, man," said Damien, shaking his head. "Whatever you want."

After that things slowly picked up.

Elijah's friends were surprisingly civil. They sat around the fire drinking while listening to music.

The alcohol made Riley's head feel light.

Elijah's hand slowly became bolder, massaging Riley's thighs then creeping into her underwear.

His touch felt good. He slipped his big fingers into her warm pussy before reaching up to rub her clit.

Riley spread her legs to give him better access. She relaxed back against his firm body and rolled her hips into his touch.

She could feel Elijah's erection growing against her back.

His warm mouth kissed her neck, working her body up to a pleasurable high.

Riley didn't care if anyone saw them.

Their attention only turned her on.

She wanted everyone to see what Elijah could do to her.

Latavia and Patrick were far more bold.

Patrick peeled the dress off Latavia's slim body, exposing her small breasts and thin hips to the cool night air. Her skin was pale and smooth like marble, but there were several red marks around her stomach and hips.

Latavia slyly glanced at Elijah to make sure he was watching.

Patrick ripped off his own shirt and pants. He was broader than Elijah with thick hair covering most of his body.

His cock was massive, making Riley wonder if it would even fit inside Latavia's small frame.

Latavia whispered something in Patrick's ear.

Patrick nodded.

He embraced Latavia, rubbing his erection against her.

They lay down in the grass together.

Patrick slid in behind Latavia and hitched one of her legs over his hip, spreading Latavia out for everyone to see.

He shoved his big dick straight between her slim legs, sinking all the way in with several small thrusts.

Latavia gasped and arched her back. She turned her head to capture Patrick's lips in a kiss.

They softly made out as Patrick slid his thick cock in and out, moaning against Latavia's mouth.

Fuck. Riley thought.

Was that supposed to turn her on?

Latavia was clearly an entitled bitch, but watching a large man fuck her senseless did strange things to Riley.

Every slide of Elijah's fingers felt ten times more intense.

It seemed like Riley wasn't the only one getting off.

All around the circle people started taking off their clothes, pressing their lips to sensitive places and joining their bodies together.

Heather was sucking on Damien's cock as he pressed his lips to her cunt, licking and sucking like they were no strangers to sex.

Elijah pressed Riley forward, peeling off her hoodie and sweatpants.

Riley didn't protest.

She felt compelled to join them. She wanted to howl and fuck under the moon.

Elijah shed his own clothes. He urged Riley onto her hands and knees then entered from behind, thrusting his big cock inside her while gripping onto her thighs.

Let them watch, Riley thought. *Let everyone know that we belong together.*

She cried out as Elijah's hard dick hit deep inside her.

Watching the sea of naked bodies and debauchery around her only increased Riley's own pleasure.

She gripped the grass under her hands as she lost control of herself.

Her mind soared through the clouds as she came hard on Elijah's dick, trembling and shaking as Elijah fucked her through the orgasm.

"Shit," he swore and pulled out, spraying his seed over Riley's naked back.

He pumped his dick as cum continued to spray forth, showering her in white fluid.

Riley shuddered.

Elijah collapsed against her once he was through. He curled their bodies together and twined his fingers through hers.

Riley pressed a lazy kiss to his lips.

This was all that she wanted.

Latavia invited another guy over. She sucked on his cock while Patrick thrust into her from behind.

The other guy climaxed with a groan, spraying his cum over Latavia's beautiful face.

Latavia's tongue darted out to lick her wet lips.

There was no shame.

Riley glanced into the forest behind them.

Its dark depths called to her.

The wolf inside her wanted to run.

Elijah looked at Riley like he knew what she was thinking.

"Do it," he whispered.

In an instant, Riley leaped to her feet, transforming into a wolf. She dashed across the clearing and into the trees, letting out a howl.

It felt amazing to finally be free.

Why had she tried to fight it?

She bounded through the leafy foliage, taking in the sights and smells around her.

Elijah wasn't far behind, running in his own wolf form.

Let's see if you're really worthy of me, Riley's inner wolf hummed, picking up the pace.

They moved deeper into the forest.

It didn't take long for Elijah's stronger body to win out.

He pounced, pinning Riley down to the forest floor and sinking his sharp teeth into her neck.

Riley howled and shoved him away, but he was soon back, holding her down.

Her body shimmied and returned to human form.

Elijah did the same.

He pressed Riley against the ground as he slid his erection straight inside her, thrusting back and forth like he wanted to break her.

"No matter where you go," he growled. "I'll always find you."

Riley shuddered with pleasure, crying out with every strong thrust of his hips.

Her new mate was strong and powerful.

He was worthy of her.

Their children would be indestructible.

"Yeah, take it all," Elijah huffed without slowing down. "You're mine now."

Riley weakly nodded, too consumed by sensation to speak.

She wanted to be bred by him.

"You like that, don't you?" Elijah said. "You're so fucking wet."

He sped up his thrusts until he came, shoving his cock in as deep as it could go, filling her fertile womb with his seed.

Yes. Riley thought while squirming against him, relishing in the aftermath of his orgasm.

Everything was wonderful.

CHAPTER NINE

Riley felt like she was drugged.

She didn't think that it was normal to become attached to someone so quickly, but she couldn't get enough of Elijah's body.

Her groin felt uncomfortable and needy when she wasn't grinding down on his dick.

It wasn't just them.

All around the school, the open fucking seemed to have magnified tenfold. Most of the classes were empty because the students were too busy screwing on the lawns.

"Well it is breeding season," Elijah said while sliding in and out of her cunt. "Isn't it like this on the outside?"

"No," Riley said. "People don't just screw wherever they want."

"That's a shame."

"No.....not really."

"We're not like them," Elijah huffed with a roll of his hips. "We have to provide a new generation in the spring. Not gonna happen unless we all work at it."

Riley nodded.

Most of what he said made no sense to her, but she was too blissed out to care.

They no longer bothered with clothes. It was much easier to shift in and out of human and wolf form without having to change.

Nobody seemed to care if Riley spent her days naked. She didn't even bother showing up for class.

Elijah openly fucked her on the cafeteria table at breakfast, spreading

Riley's legs wide to drill his dick deep inside.

"You go Elijah!" cheered a guy walking past. "Fill her up like a pro."

"Yeah, I'll fill her up," Elijah growled, rocking his hips back and forth. "She's gonna have my cum dripping from her pussy for a week."

Riley shuddered at his words, rolling her hips to get more stimulation against her clit.

Latavia only rolled her eyes.

She'd become increasingly bold since Elijah rejected her, jumping from one male friend to another. Often screwing two at the same time.

She sat sandwiched between Damien and Patrick. One kissed her mouth while the other pressed his lips to her neck, working one hand between her thighs to rub at her clit.

It was obvious that she was trying to make Elijah jealous, but he didn't seem to care.

He was too busy being with Riley to give a damn about what Latavia did.

Wanda's cousin Tommy was also there across the room, receiving a blowjob from a large dark haired girl.

Riley's classmate Davis was laid out on a table like a buffet. An older student was riding his cock as another fucked his mouth.

Mr. Bites merrily greeted him as he walked past.

Riley scanned the room for Wanda, but she was nowhere in sight.

Riley could only assume that she was too busy tied up on Jimmy's cock.

She turned her attention back to Elijah, trying to pretend that Wanda's absence from her life didn't sting.

"Have you ever heard of fated mates?" asked Elijah that evening.

They were both lying on the grass looking up at the moon. Fresh cum from their last round was smeared across Riley's thighs.

"No," she said. "What's that?"

"I heard that if you meet your fated mate you instantly know." He nervously ran a hand through the damp grass beside his leg. "That's how I feel when I'm with you."

Those words made Riley's heart swoon.

She thought of her own strange compulsion to constantly be around him.

"Yeah, me too," Riley said. "I feel the same."

Elijah rolled his body on top of hers, joining their hands together then slipping his cock inside.

He slowly rocked in and out, trying to savor the sensation.

Riley trembled around him.

She wished that moment would last forever.

Elijah pressed a kiss to her neck. "I want you to meet my mother."

"Your mother?" Riley gasped.

She wished that he could have picked a better time to bring it up.

"Yeah," Elijah huffed. "She'll be at school tomorrow. You're important to me, so I want her to know about you."

"Okay," Riley nodded.

She wanted to make him happy.

Elijah's mouth curved up into a smile.

He pulled out, causing Riley to let out a groan of protest, until he moved down her body, pressing his lips to her clit.

Riley jolted.

That was something new.

Elijah took hold of her thighs to spread her legs further, licking and sucking her sex.

Riley groaned and rolled her hips against his lips.

It felt amazing.

His wet tongue was heavenly against her pulsing apex, stimulating her in ways that she'd never experienced before.

There were still so many things that they had left to try.

"Delicious," Elijah murmured against her cunt.

He took a long swipe with his tongue.

Riley swore and gripped his hair.

It was too much.

Elijah's mouth was all she could think of.

Pressure grew in her lower body until it exploded, leaving Riley trembling and shaking as she struggled for breath.

Elijah diligently licked her until she was through.

Riley squirmed away from his touch when it became too much.

Elijah climbed over her body and pressed his cock back inside her, basking in the added lubrication caused by her orgasm.

He pressed his face to her neck, shuddering as the pleasure consumed him. "We're going to be so happy."

Riley nodded and wrapped her arms around his neck, holding him close as he came deep inside her.

CHAPTER TEN

The next morning, Riley dressed in her best clothes, a blue summer dress and white cardigan that once belonged to Wanda's mother.

The dress was two sizes too large, but she managed to fix it by placing a belt over her waist. She then styled her hair up into a high ponytail.

Riley checked her reflection in the mirror.

It was far more plain and reserved than her usual style, but hopefully Elijah's mother would like it.

"It's fine." Elijah wrapped his arms around her waist and kissed the back of her head. "We'll only see her for a moment."

"What's she like?" Riley asked.

"Strict. And maybe a little too overprotective, but she needs to understand that this is my life not hers."

"Sounds like she cares about you a lot."

"Yeah. I guess you could say that. What about your mother?"

Riley bit her lower lip. She didn't like talking about her family, but if she and Elijah were a couple then he deserved to know.

"We were close when I was a kid," said Riley. "But things changed a lot after she remarried. I doubt that she's noticed that I'm missing."

"Oh," said Elijah like he didn't know what to say.

There it is, Riley thought.

People usually reacted that way whenever she explained her family situation.

"Don't worry about it," Riley said with a forced smile. "Today's about you, not me."

She took hold of Elijah's hand and pulled him out of the room.

They made their way to the principal's office.

Elijah was quieter than normal. He kept rubbing his face like a nervous tick.

"So why is your mom even here?" Riley asked.

"My family made a donation to the school," said Elijah. "So she came to talk to them about it in person, and to see me of course," he added with a wink.

A donation? she thought.

Riley knew that Elijah's family had to be well off by the way that he dressed, but it sounded like they were richer than she imagined.

He certainly was a good catch.

They arrived at the staff room. It was mostly empty, except for a young brunette secretary who sat at a desk by the door.

She smiled at Elijah, but then raised an eyebrow when she saw Riley.

"Morning Elijah," said the secretary. "Are you here to see your mother?"

"Yes," said Elijah. "Is she here yet?"

"Just in the principal's office." She pointed to a room behind her. "They already finished, but she stuck around to see you.

"Thanks," Elijah nodded and pulled Riley along with him.

This is it, Riley thought. *It's now or never.*

Elijah pushed open the door.

His mother sat on a green sofa by the wall. An empty cup of tea sat on a coffee table before her.

She was younger than Riley expected. In her late thirties or maybe forty.

She was slim and elegant with perfect nails and several gold bands around her thin wrists.

Her pale blonde hair was styled back into a tight bun, and her skirt and jacket didn't look cheap.

She could have been a model or a movie star.

But her expression was terrifying.

Even though her own son was right before her, she didn't look pleased.

"Elijah," she said. "I honestly expected a lot better from you. Since when did you start hanging out with muncher garbage?"

Riley was too shocked for words.

Who the fuck was this woman?

Elijah seemed to think that he could still salvage the situation.

"Mother." He tightly gripped Riley's hand. "This is my girlfriend, Riley."

Riley wanted to run, but she stayed firm, for Elijah's sake.

Maybe it was just a misunderstanding?

Elijah's mother raked her eyes over Riley, then let out a disappointed sigh.

"I suppose that there isn't anything that I can do to stop you." She picked up her handbag to check her phone. "Just make sure not to infect Latavia with any strange muncher diseases."

"Mother-"

"And make sure that your grandfather doesn't find out that you've been mixing generations of elite breeding with....this *thing*."

Riley thought that Elijah would at least stand up for her, but instead he sadly looked down at his feet.

"Yes, mother," he obediently replied.

Riley couldn't believe what was happening.

Was he seriously going to just stand there and take it?

"Now, I've been talking to Latavia's family," said Elijah's mother. "And they want to set your wedding for next June. You can at least manage that, can't you?"

"Yes, mother," Elijah replied.

No way!

"Wait-" Riley tried to protest, but Elijah squeezed her hand to stop her.

Don't, he mouthed at her.

"Good," Elijah's mother picked up her handbag and stood to her feet. "I'll send you more details once we work them out."

She walked straight past them to the door, tall heels clicking against the wooden floor.

She paused to take one last look at Riley. "Elijah, we've let you have your fun, but don't forget what's expected of you."

"Yeah," Elijah muttered, tall shoulders slouching with defeat. "I know."

"Cheer up." She kissed him on the cheek. "I'll prepare all your favorites next time you visit home."

With a small wave, she exited through the door, leaving Elijah and Riley alone in the room.

Riley could no longer contain herself.

"What the hell was that?" she blurted out.

"What was what?" Elijah rubbed his temples.

"All that stuff about you and Latavia getting married. Not to mention how she clearly hates me."

"She doesn't hate you...she just...doesn't really know you. And as for Latavia...."

"You need to tell her that you don't want to get married."

"But I have to marry Latavia."

"What!"

"It's already been decided."

Riley felt like he'd slapped her in the face.

He didn't want a future with her.

He had his whole life planned out from the very beginning.

Riley wanted to claw his face off. "Then why did you feed me all that shit about being together if you plan on marrying Latavia?"

"Look..I..I.." Elijah struggled to get the right words out. "You and I will be together, but I'll just also be married to Latavia, that's all."

"This morning she was screwing two other guys."

"Well.....she's also free to be with whoever she wants."

"So this marriage is just for show while you screw around with other people?"

"We'll have to sleep together sometimes too. My family expects us to have more children."

It felt like the ground suddenly disappeared from under Riley's feet.

She struggled to breathe. "More children? Don't tell me that you already have..."

Riley didn't have to finish the question because she could tell from Elijah's face that it was true.

She shouldn't have been surprised. Everyone else around her already had several kids.

"How many..." It was hard to get the question out. "How many children do you have?"

Elijah crossed his arms. His gaze fell to the floor. "Two with Latavia... Another two with other girls."

"Seriously?" Riley snapped.

"The elders set it up. They wanted us to start young, you know..... to help increase the werewolf population."

"Oh," Riley said sarcastically. "So that they can take over the world?"

"Something like that."

There was so much more that she wanted to ask, but Riley knew that she wouldn't like the answers.

It was obvious that their relationship was doomed from the very beginning.

She had been used.

"I don't fucking believe this," Riley muttered. "Enjoy your life with Latavia."

She moved to the door but Elijah blocked her way.

"Wait!" He placed his hands on her shoulders to stop her. "I meant everything I said. I want us to be together."

"Let go of me!" Riley shoved him away.

"Riley!"

"I never want to see your stupid face again!" she snapped then stormed out of the room.

Her eyes burned.

Riley fought back tears as she dashed down the hall.

The illusion was broken.

It felt like she'd been flung from heaven and back down to earth.

She didn't know Elijah.

The image that she had created for him in her head wasn't real.

She had been living in her own fantasy world.

Riley flung open the door to her room. She collapsed onto her bed, burying her face in her hands as the tears fell.

She had believed him.

She thought that he loved her.

How had she allowed herself to get so carried away?

The old her wouldn't have so easily jumped into bed with a guy she didn't know.

Had all the werewolf hormones turned her into an idiot?

"Riley? said Wanda's voice from the door. "Are you okay?"

Riley looked up to see Wanda standing before her. Her bare legs were smudged with dirt like she had been out in the forest.

Seeing her friend again only made Riley cry harder.

"Hey." Wanda took a place beside Riley on the bed, putting a comforting arm around her shoulders. "What's wrong?"

"I don't belong here," Riley sobbed.

"What do you mean?"

"I thought that I could handle it." Riley's voice hitched. "But I can't. I don't know who I am anymore. I just want to go home."

Wanda silently rubbed Riley's back, patiently waiting for her to cry it out.

"Have you been feeling this way for a while?"

"Yes."

"I'm not sure how to help you, but I know someone who might."

"Who?"

"This guy we once helped. He hated this place too, but he found somewhere else. Maybe I can ask him to come pick you up."

Riley nodded. She'd do anything to get away.

"I'll give him a call." Wanda pulled her phone out and stood to her feet.

Riley waited while Wanda talked on the phone.

Riley packed the few things she owned into a small backpack. They were miles from town, but she was leaving whether or not anyone came to pick her up.

"He's coming," said Wanda. "He'll be a few hours, but he said to come meet him halfway down the mountain."

"Do you trust this guy?"

"Yeah, he's nice, even if he's a little strange."

Riley couldn't believe how eager Wanda was to help, even after Riley had treated her friend like crap.

"I'm sorry," said Riley. "I could tell how you wanted to warn me about Elijah, but I ignored you."

"It's okay. I understand that sometimes there's no stopping these things."

"But I was a bitch to you, Wanda."

"Really?" Wanda smiled. "I never noticed."

Riley couldn't tell if her friend was joking or not.

"To be honest, Tommy was more disappointed than me," Wanda continued. "He was convinced that the two of you would make the cutest babies."

Riley gagged.

"He even had names picked out and everything," said Wanda. "Cesar, Augustus, Sparticus-"

"Please never mention that again."

Wanda let out a laugh. She picked up Riley's backpack. "We better get going. It's a long walk."

CHAPTER ELEVEN

It was a long trek down the mountain in human form.

Wanda said that it would be faster if they transformed into wolves, but Riley didn't trust herself.

She knew that the wolf inside her still longed for Elijah. She was certain that it would go seek him out if it had a chance.

Her animal side didn't seem to care how fucked up their relationship was.

Riley needed to get as far away from him as possible.

After an hour of walking, they arrived at a run down shack by the side of the road. Most of the ceiling had collapsed and the wooden walls were overgrown with vines.

"I can wait with you if you like," said Wanda.

Riley looked up at the overcast sky. It was already sprinkling with rain.

"No, you should go. It looks like it's going to pour down soon."

"Are you sure?"

"I traveled the country alone for months. I think that I can handle this."

"But last time you got turned into a werewolf?"

"Which means that it can't happen again."

Wanda embraced Riley. "Take good care of yourself, okay."

Riley nodded, fighting back tears. "Thanks for everything you did to help me. Without you, I would still be running around the woods thinking that I was a wolf."

"I'm sure that you would have pulled yourself together eventually."

"I highly doubt that."

"You need to have more faith in yourself."

Riley pulled away and took hold of Wanda's shoulders, looking her straight in the eyes.

"You should break up with Jimmy," said Riley. "That guy's no good for you. You're smart and kind and you deserve so much better than him."

"Hey, he's not that bad."

"I've seen plenty of guys like him, and it never ends well."

"We'll see." Wanda gave her a sad smile and stepped away. "I'll think about it."

"You're more than just a breeding machine," said Riley. "No matter what they want you to think."

"I know that." Wanda winked. "Maybe I'm the one who's just working the system to get all the free orgasms?"

Riley couldn't help her mouth from breaking out into a grin.

Wanda backed away towards the forest. "Look me up if you're ever in this neck of the woods."

"Make sure to call if you ever leave to live in the human world!"

"Goodbye, Riley."

"See you later, Wanda."

Wanda waved at Riley until she disappeared behind the trees, leaving Riley alone.

The sky opened up soon after Wanda left.

Riley took shelter under what was left of the shack roof, watching the rain pour down.

Being alone was dangerous.

She couldn't help but think of *him*.

Even after everything that happened, she still thought of going back.

Maybe they could make it work.

Elijah would marry Latavia, but he and Riley could still date on the side. They'd spend time together when he wasn't busy impregnating his stuck-up wife.

Elijah's mother was a bitch and Riley's children would probably be brainwashed by a crazy sex cult, but maybe it wouldn't be so bad.

The more Riley thought about it, the more ridiculous it seemed.

It wasn't the life that she wanted.

She could never go back.

Riley's nose twitched as she sensed a presence behind the trees.

She wasn't alone.

"I know that you're there," Riley said.

Elijah emerged before her, soaked from the rain. His blonde hair was plastered to his forehead as he sadly gazed at her.

"I'm sorry," said Elijah, voice trembling. "Please come back."

"I can't." Riley's eyes burned, but she managed to hold back the tears. "It's never going to work."

"I'll talk to my mother. I'll tell her to call off the wedding."

"It's not just that." Riley found it difficult to look at him. "There are so many other things."

"Like what?"

"We barely know each other. I only met you two weeks ago."

"But we're fated mates."

"That's just a fantasy."

"But it feels real to me."

"There's this thing called the *honeymoon period*, Elijah." Riley clenched her hands into fists. "It makes you more attracted to your partner in a new relationship, but it fades with time."

He shook his head. "No, it won't."

"Yes, it will. You'll get tired of me and move onto another girl. Just like you did to Latavia."

"No. I know that my feelings won't change."

As torn up as he appeared, Riley refused to believe him. "But you don't even like people who used to be human?"

"I like you."

"But you hate what I am?"

"It doesn't matter when we're together."

"You already have children.

"And what's wrong with that?"

"Do you even know them?"

"They're with the elders."

"And you're okay with that?"

"It's what everyone does."

"That's just crap that those people have fed you. You're in a fucking cult, Elijah."

"No! It's not like that!"

"If I asked you to leave this place would you do it? Would you come live with me in the human world?"

Elijah was silent for a moment, but then shook his head.

"That's what I thought," Riley muttered.

"You should come back with me," said Elijah. "You're not human anymore. You belong here. We can help you be better."

"Just go, Elijah," Riley begged. "Please let me go home."

Elijah didn't budge. "Please-"

"Just go!"

The look on Elijah's face was almost enough to break her, but Riley remained firm.

She wouldn't be like her mother. She wouldn't let an entitled arsehole run her life.

Elijah sadly lowered his head and walked away, but he stopped to take one last look at her.

"I just want you to know," said Elijah. "That I meant everything I said, even if you didn't."

And with that he turned and disappeared.

Riley bit her lower lip, fighting the urge to call out to Elijah.

It felt like he took a piece of her heart with him.

A white pick up truck appeared on the road an hour later.

Riley pulled herself together and got to her feet.

It parked beside the shack.

A thin guy in denim overalls emerged from the driver's seat. He looked to be in his mid twenties with long ash blonde hair and a goatee.

"Riley, right?" He held out his hand. "I'm Scott."

"Riley," she said before realizing that he already knew that.

Scott didn't pull her up on her mistake.

"Let's hit the road," he said. "I bet that you can't wait to be rid of this place."

"Yeah," said Riley. She moved around the truck and hopped into the passenger seat. "Let's go."

Scott got behind the wheel and started the engine, slowly pulling out onto the road.

Riley watched the mountain scenery speed past them from the window.

Elijah wasn't beside her, but she felt hope again for the first time in weeks.

Everything would get better with time.

She had the rest of her life to work on it.

WEREWOLF
BREEDING
ACADEMY 2

BY BEATRIX ARDEN

CHAPTER ONE

"He said that if I became a werewolf, then we could be together," Abigail sobbed, tears running down her pale freckled cheeks. "But after he bit me...he took me to his compound...where I met...his six other wives!"

Her words became incomprehensible as she broke down, sobbing about her ex-boyfriend's atrocities.

She looked tiny in the large leather armchair, surrounded by cheap junk store furniture and faded throw rugs.

Abigail's wispy blonde hair was a mess, and there were several scratches up her thin legs. Her short pink dress looked like it belonged in a club, and her heels were covered in dirt.

Riley crossed her legs.

The old metal chair groaned under her weight.

Unlike Abigail, Riley was dressed more practically in a pair of worn jeans and a gray sweater.

Her long black hair was pulled back, and her face was bare without a hint of makeup.

There were faint lines around her dark eyes which made her look older.

Riley blamed it on stress.

Abigail paused to gasp for breath. "And then...he wanted me to have sex with him and this other woman," she sobbed. "But she was actually his cousin...and they wanted me to have their babies."

Scott coughed to clear his throat, trying to keep his face neutral. He crossed his arms and leaned back against his battered desk.

His style was a cross between *lumberjack* and *hipster*. He was wearing thick black glasses and a red checkered shirt. Long blonde hair flowed freely down his shoulders.

"What matters is you're here now." Scott passed Abigail a tissue. "You're in a safe place and we can get you the help that you need."

Abigail nodded while wiping tears from her face.

"Right, Riley?" said Scott.

"Yes." Riley tried to put on a reassuring smile. "Yes, of course. You never have to worry about that stupid guy again."

"You can stay here tonight," said Scott. "Then in the morning we'll get you some medication. Things may be hard now, but you'll be back to normal before long."

Abigail's lower lip trembled.

Scott barely had any warning before the young woman launched herself at him, embracing Scott in a tight hug.

"Thank you," Abigail cried, resting her face against his neck. Her short dress slipped up to unveil her lace underwear. "You're the nicest guy that I've ever met!"

Riley rolled her eyes.

Abigail had been through a lot, but Riley was certain that the young woman was only using the hug as an excuse to get a whiff of Scott's scent. It wasn't unusual for werewolves.

If Scott wasn't careful, Abigail could end up getting too attached.

"I have some clothes that you can wear, Abigail," said Riley. "We could go pick them up now, right Scott?"

"Yeah, sure." Scott gave Abigail an awkward pat on the back before gently pushing her away.

"You're leaving me?" Abigail whined, lower lip trembling like she was going to burst into tears again.

"We'll be back soon," said Scott. "Bathroom's in the back. Why don't you go take a shower while you wait?"

"Okay." Abigail lowered her head.

"Don't worry," said Scott. "We won't abandon you."

Abigail launched herself at Scott again, sobbing against his shirt.

"I was so scared!" she wailed, like a small child.

Scott patted her back while trying to pry her shaking fingers from his forearms.

Despite Abigail's scantily clad outfit, she was just a vulnerable young woman. No different to the other people they had helped over the years.

Riley decided to give them a moment alone.

She walked through Scott's house to his truck.

Scott had leased the property to help people who were dealing with their werewolf transformations.

The house was an old five bedroom vacation home. It hadn't been renovated in years, so the door hinges had rusted and the wallpaper was turning yellow.

Nobody seemed to mind because they didn't stay long.

Scott emerged out the front door a few minutes later. His shirt was covered in several damp patches and hints of snot.

"Thanks for your help," he said. "Having you there really encouraged her to open up."

"But I barely did anything," said Riley.

"But I think having another woman there really put her at ease." Scott unlocked his truck and slipped in behind the driver's wheel. "A lot of girls like her have trouble trusting men."

Riley opened the door and sat down in the passenger seat.

But she didn't seem to have any problems, Riley thought. *She didn't hesitate to throw herself all over you like you were her next meal.*

Scott started the engine and pulled out onto the road. "I'll probably stop by to pick up some dinner on the way back. You're welcome to come too if you want."

"I should really get back." Riley tapped her fingers against the window. "Trissy's been bugging me not to stay out too late."

"Still obsessing over everything?"

"You have no idea," Riley groaned. "Sometimes she treats me like I'm one of her children."

Scott let out a quiet chuckle, causing Riley to roll her eyes.

She glanced out the window to watch the scenery speed past.

When Riley imagined living by the sea, she thought of palm trees and pristine white beaches, but East Cove was nothing like that.

Overlooked by most tourists, it was a small coastal town with grey skies and freezing cold water.

It was full of cheaply built holiday homes and people who were looking for a quiet place to retire or hide.

It was perfect for someone like Riley.

Five years earlier, Riley was bitten by a werewolf while traveling alone. Luckily she was helped by a young woman named Wanda, but the cult Wanda introduced Riley to was far from a barrel of fun.

It was nothing more than a set up to encourage young werewolves to breed with each other, allowing them to shamelessly screw all over the halls and forest.

It was too much for Riley. She didn't last more than a few weeks.

Luckily Wanda put her in touch with Scott, who was kind enough to save her from that madhouse.

He introduced Riley to a new way of living which suited her much better. She had finally regained some semblance of a human life.

Riley tapped her fingers against the truck window. "Have you heard anything from Wanda?"

Scott shook his head. "No, but she often goes dark when she starts things up with a new guy. You know what werewolves are like. They don't tend to update their status online."

Riley bit her lip. She knew that Scott was probably right, but that didn't stop her from worrying. "You don't think that anything could have happened to her?"

"I doubt it. Wanda's pretty good at looking after herself, and she's got plenty of people watching her back."

"But still..."

"Wanda's spent her whole life around werewolves. She knows how to work the system better than you think."

"Yeah... I suppose..."

Riley tried to push her concerns to the back of her mind.

Wanda helped Riley the most after she first turned into a werewolf. Riley still felt like she owed the other woman a great debt.

Scott turned onto a narrow dirt road. Untamed bushes and tree branches scratched the sides of the vehicle.

After several winding turns, they pulled up before an old farmstead.

The large house had been built sixty years earlier. White paint was peeling from the wooden boards, and there were several tiles missing from the roof.

It was surrounded by overgrown fields and dark forests. Several goats roamed free in a paddock, and there was a small vegetable garden.

A group of children and wolves were playing outside, chasing each other in circles.

One boy bounded towards them in wolf form, seamlessly transforming into a human mid-jump.

It was Trissy's son Jacob. The ten year old was tall for his age with freckled skin and flaming red hair.

"What's she like?" Jacob asked with boundless enthusiasm. "Is she nice? Is she gonna come live with us?"

Scott reached out to ruffle Jacob's hair. "It's too early to say. Abigail might want to get back to her family soon."

"I hope that she comes here." Jacob smiled. "Then we'd have someone else to help with the chores. Mama's always complaining that the house is a mess."

"Aren't there already enough of you here," said Scott. "You might have to give up your bed."

"There's plenty of space in the shed," said Jacob. "Except when Vanessa brings her friends over. They're always super loud and screaming and-"

"Okay. Okay," coughed Scott. "I'll let you know what Abigail thinks."

Jacob's face broke out into a giant grin. He spun on his heels and transformed back into a brown wolf, rejoining the game.

Despite Jacob's enthusiasm, Riley highly doubted that Abigail would stick around for long.

Abigail had at least been smart enough to get an IUD before the crazy wolf fucking began.

Scott would hook Abigail up with some decent meds, then she'd be back clubbing in the city with her besties within a few weeks.

Riley was an entirely different story.

It would be years before she could return to regular human society.

Running amongst the children was a smaller wolf pup with jet black fur. He caught sight of Riley and bounded towards her.

He transformed into a small child with pale skin, black hair, and piercing blue eyes.

He attached himself to Riley's leg, hugging her tightly.

"Hey, Ryan," Riley said with a smile, running her fingers through his soft dark hair. "Did you miss me?"

Ryan silently looked up at her with his wide eyes. He gave Riley a small smile before running off to rejoin the game.

"Still not talking?" asked Scott.

"No," said Riley, failing to suppress a familiar sense of guilt. "Nothing that really sounds like a word anyway."

"It's okay," said Scott. "Some kids just take longer than others."

"Yeah, I know," said Riley, even though she didn't believe him.

Her son was four. He should be talking already.

Instead he just made animal-like growls and exaggerated hand gestures.

Riley often thought of taking him to a doctor, but Ryan was still too unpredictable. He preferred being a wolf more than human and it was difficult to make him wear clothes.

He didn't seem to understand that people outside the farmstead wouldn't take kindly to werewolves.

Ryan was Riley's souvenir from her time in a werewolf cult.

Before becoming a werewolf, Riley was meticulously careful about birth control, but that was all thrown out the window once a wild animal was shoved into her skull.

Her inner wolf only wanted to screw as much as possible, obsessed with getting knocked up and pumping out babies in the spring.

Riley was too immersed in a sex induced haze to worry about the consequences of her love-making with Ryan's father.

Riley tore her eyes away from her son. "I'll just go grab those clothes for Abigail."

"Okay," said Scott. "I'll wait out here."

Riley walked up to the battered front door and entered the house.

The interior hadn't been renovated since they started renting the place. It stank of cigarette smoke and the floors were littered with children's toys.

Riley had only taken several steps when Trissy suddenly appeared.

Trissy was only in her mid-thirties, but raising seven children had taken its toll on her health.

Her face was lined with wrinkles and her curly brown hair was streaked with gray. She was dressed in a frumpy T-shirt and jeans stained with paint.

"You forgot to do the dishes again," she said robotically like she was too exhausted to show an ounce of emotion.

"I'm sorry," said Riley. "Scott needed my help with some things."

"Do them," Trissy said. "Do them soon. It's not fair on the rest of us if you keep letting your chores slide."

"I'll do it in a moment," said Riley. "I just need to give Scott some things."

Trissy stared into space for a moment as though caught in a daze.

She was snapped out of it by her twin sons fighting in front of the T.V.

"Change it!" Trissy's five year old son Micheal screamed at his brother while trying to rip the remote out of the other boy's hand.

"No!" Thomas yelled back and kicked his brother in the stomach. "It's mine!"

"Give it to me!"

"No!"

"It's mine!"

"No!"

"Mom!"

"Just stop it," Trissy moaned and went to stop the fighting. "If you can't work it out amongst yourselves, then I'm taking the T.V. away."

Riley slipped into her room.

She shared it with Ryan, so several of his paintings and drawings were pinned to the walls. The floor was covered in plastic cars and trucks.

Riley and Ryan each had their own beds, but they shared the wardrobe and chest of drawers.

Riley went through the wardrobe in search of anything that she didn't need. She pulled out several old shirts and two pairs of jeans.

She slipped them into a plastic bag, then went outside to meet Scott.

Scott had immersed himself in a game of tag, chasing the kids around while making exaggerated monster sounds.

"Scotty wolf is looking for dinner," Scott growled in a low voice while waving his arms in the air.

"Wolf! Wolf! Wolf!" the children chanted together.

Scott reached for his shirt to pull it over his head, but then looked up to see Riley standing there.

"Maybe next time, guys." He pried a small child from his arm and walked over to Riley.

"Here." Riley handed him the clothes. "I don't know what Abigail likes, but hopefully they fit."

"Thanks," said Scott. "I'm sure she'll appreciate it."

"Let me know if you need help with anything else."

"I should be okay. I'll give you a call if anything comes up."

"I can stop by after my shift tomorrow." Riley nervously shifted her weight. "Check in to see how she's doing?"

"Really." Scott smiled. "That would be great."

"Dishes!" Trissy yelled out from inside.

Riley cringed.

"Better let you go," Scott chuckled. "Wouldn't want to keep mother waiting."

"Please," Riley huffed. "She's barely old enough to be my mother."

Scott backed away towards his truck. "I'll pick you up from work tomorrow."

"Sounds good." Riley waved goodbye. "Catch you then."

Scott got in his truck and started the engine, slowly reversing back onto the road.

Riley went straight to the kitchen, horrified by the massive pile of dirty dishes sitting in the sink.

It had only been a day, but with so many people in the house they quickly stacked up.

Trissy wouldn't be able to serve dinner until Riley finished cleaning at least half.

She sighed and turned on the tap, slowly washing the plates and glasses one by one.

The screams of the children playing outside wafted in from the open kitchen door.

Ryan was being chased by Trissy's youngest daughter Andrea, a bright energetic toddler who hadn't inherited the werewolf gene.

Andrea still hadn't worked out that she was never going to turn into a wolf. She spent most of her days following her older siblings around while making growling noises.

As a child born from werewolves, she was also immune from werewolf bites. She'd never become a werewolf even if her siblings gnawed on her all day.

Riley considered Andrea lucky. The small girl had a chance at living a regular human life.

Riley would have given up an arm if it meant that Ryan could have the same.

Trissy's oldest daughter Mia was also born human. She sat on the veranda immersed in her phone, bored like she'd already witnessed enough werewolf shit to last her a lifetime.

The kitchen door swung open and Vanessa walked through.

Vanessa was the same age as Trissy, but she appeared years younger with shiny black hair that fell to her waist, long tanned legs, and full lips covered in dark lipstick. She was wearing a short purple dress that hugged her curvy frame, along with a black leather jacket.

Vanessa pulled open the fridge and took out a small tub of yogurt.

"Was that Scotty out there?" she asked.

"Yes," said Riley. "He asked me to help him out with a new girl."

"Oh."

Riley put down the dish she was holding. "What do you mean *oh*?"

"Nothing," said Vanessa.

"Really?"

"It's just.." Vanessa pulled a spoon out of a drawer. "I can never tell if he's into you, or just wants to be your bestie."

Riley's heart skipped a beat.

"Scott's nice to everyone," Riley said while trying her best to remain composed.

"Don't get me wrong, we all know that Scotty gets high off appreciation." Vanessa took a seat at the table and started eating yogurt from the tub. "But you're gonna have to make a move before some needy bitch digs his claws into him."

Riley cringed. "It's not like that."

"So you don't find him attractive?"

"No."

"Not even a little?"

Riley bit her lower lip.

It was hard to explain.

Scott was great. He was everything she should want in a boyfriend, but whenever Riley imagined doing anything more than hugging, she was met with a mental block, like her mind refused to accept the possibility.

Whenever Riley imagined sex, all thoughts led straight back to Ryan's father.

She scrubbed at one plate far harder than necessary. "Nothing is going to happen between us."

Vanessa rolled her eyes.

"It's been years since you had that kid, but you still refuse to date anyone." Vanessa licked the back of the spoon. "When are you going to get out there again?"

"I will," said Riley. "Maybe once Ryan gets older."

"Like how old?"

"Eighteen."

Vanessa laughed. "Your pussy will be dryer than Trissy's by then."

"No it won't," Riley muttered. "I just don't want Ryan to go through what I did growing up. I didn't like any of my step parents."

"I'm not saying that you have to marry anyone," said Vanessa. "Just go out and have fun every once in a while. I could introduce you to some guys I know."

"No, thank you," Riley quickly replied.

All of Vanessa's hook-ups tended to be older men with weird beastiality kinks.

Trissy forbade Vanessa from bringing any more men into the house. They were only allowed in the shed.

Riley had heard plenty of things from the *sex shed* that she'd rather forget.

"Okay, suit yourself." Vanessa walked out of the kitchen. "But the offer is always open."

"Okay." Riley sighed. "I'll keep that in mind."

Vanessa was probably right, but Riley didn't feel the need to date anyone.

She was far too busy trying to sort out the fallout from her last relationship.

When Riley found out that she was pregnant, she thought that raising the baby alone would be the right thing to do.

Her own mother was a single parent for years, so Riley thought that she could do it too.

She planned to work and go back to school part-time, but raising a child was far harder than she ever imagined, not to mention one who was also a werewolf.

Asking her family to help was out of the question, so she only had Scott, Trissy and Vanessa to fall back on. There was barely any work in East Cove, so her crappy part-time job wasn't enough to afford rent.

Looking after Ryan took up the rest of her time.

It was too dangerous to put him in a regular school, so she had to homeschool him herself. It would be years before Riley could even think of going to college.

She was stuck as a single mother living below the poverty line.

She had escaped werewolf society and entered her own personal hell.

Riley's eyes burned, but she held back the tears.

She refused to let anyone catch her crying.

She'd stay strong. For Ryan's sake.

CHAPTER TWO

In her dreams, Riley was back at the academy.

She wandered through the forest surrounding the school. The trees were ghostly white. Dark shadows danced back and forth. The howling of wolves echoed around her.

It was like the last five years never happened.

Elijah's naked body towered over hers, unchanged from the day that they parted.

His smooth pale skin gleamed in the moonlight and his large muscles radiated strength.

His short blonde hair was wild and his deep blue eyes were fixated on her.

Elijah's naked body pressed against Riley's as his large cock slowly moved in and out of her dripping pussy.

Riley moaned and wrapped her arms around his neck to draw him closer, basking in the warmth from his naked body.

Addictive pleasure grew in her core with every slow thrust of his hips.

"*Don't you see?*" Elijah whispered. "I said that we would always be together."

Elijah opened his mouth wide, then clamped down hard on Riley's neck, pressing down until his sharp teeth pierced her skin.

Blood spilled forth from the wound.

Riley wanted to scream, but the wolf inside her felt nothing but joy.

Her pussy fluttered around his dick as she came, sucking him deeper, encouraging Elijah to flood her warm body with his seed.

Yes, this was right.

This was what they were meant to be.

Riley jolted awake, gasping for breath.

Early morning rays of light filtered across her bedroom.

She was at home, in her own bed, not in the middle of a creepy forest hundreds of miles away.

Ryan was curled up asleep on the other side of the room. He had fallen asleep in wolf form. His small furry body moved up and down with each gentle breath.

Riley ran her fingers along her neck, expecting to feel blood, but it was smooth without any marks.

It was just a dream.

Riley pressed a hand to her chest as she tried to calm her racing heart.

Sex dreams about Ryan's father were nothing new.

They happened at least once a week, mostly reliving several scenarios from their doomed relationship.

Riley always freaked out the moment that she awoke, afraid that she'd find him asleep next to her.

It was only a dream, Riley tried to reassure herself. *He doesn't know where I am.*

He probably wouldn't even care.

Riley slipped out of bed.

She moved to the bathroom and opened the medicine cabinet above the sink.

She reached for the top shelf and pulled out a large bottle full of white pills, taking two out, then swallowing them with a glass of water.

As long as she took the medication every day she'd be fine.

The pills occasionally gave her headaches, but they kept the creepy werewolf urges at bay. She hadn't even transformed in years.

The medicine had been around for decades, but no one in the werewolf cult even bothered to mention it. They were much happier trying to integrate Riley into their society and use her as breeding stock.

Riley returned to her room and got dressed for the day.

Riley caught a bus into town.

Her part-time job was at a small cafe on the main street.

The narrow building was wedged between a small supermarket and a shoe store. The beach was just a small walk away, so it was busy during the summer.

The owner was a fan of antiques, so the old furniture and rustic interior made it look older. The walls were covered in black and white photos of the town from sixty years earlier.

The back of the store was taken up by a large counter, an expensive coffee machine, and a glass case full of cakes and sandwiches.

It was quiet before ten, so Riley usually worked her morning shifts alone.

That day was no exception. The cafe was empty except for a few retirees and people stopping by to get takeout.

"A large hot mocha without coffee," ordered one elderly woman dressed in a grey tracksuit. Her thick make-up made her face appear orange.

"So you'd like a hot chocolate?" asked Riley from behind the counter.

"No, I asked for a mocha without coffee," the woman snapped back.

"Don't you mean a mocha with decaf, dear?" asked her elderly partner, a balding man dressed in a matching grey tracksuit.

"That's what I just said!" the woman snapped back.

Her partner rolled his eyes.

Riley let out a small smile and wrote the order down on her notepad. "Okay, one large hot decaf mocha."

Riley took the woman's money, then handed them a number.

The couple went and sat down on a leather sofa at the front of the shop.

Riley moved to the other side of the counter to make the drink, pulling various ingredients out of the small fridge under the counter.

The bell above the door rattled as a new customer entered the store. Their slow footsteps echoed as they approached.

"I'll be with you in a moment," Riley said as she finished making the drink, turning to take it over to the elderly couple.

She jumped with shock, spilling half the beverage down her apron.

"Hello, Riley," said Elijah.

Riley froze. Her panicked mind found it difficult to believe that it was really Ryan's father standing before her.

Elijah hadn't changed much in five years.

His short blond hair was neatly combed back and his lower face was freshly shaved. He was dressed in a designer jacket with equally expensive looking shoes.

He still had the same pale skin and piercing blue eyes that she clearly remembered, but there were faint wrinkles around his face that hadn't been there years earlier.

He looked more mature, but the shadows around his eyes were deeper than before.

It was something that Riley could relate to.

She could feel her body reacting to Elijah's proximity. A cold shiver ran down her spine and her arms broke out in goosebumps.

There was a stirring in her groin, but it was less intense than before, as though her senses had been numbed.

Him...

"Riley?" Elijah asked softly.

She quickly put down the mug, then grabbed a towel and patted down her wet apron.

Fuck, she swore to herself as her face turned red.

She'd just made an idiot of herself in front of Elijah.

"I'm sorry. It's a surprise for me too." Elijah nervously laughed. "Meeting here like this after so many years."

"Yeah." Riley forced herself to laugh in a poor attempt to salvage the situation. "What brings you here?"

"I was just passing through," said Elijah. "But then I caught hints of your scent nearby."

Of course. He's a werewolf, Riley thought. *Damn them and their super noses.*

"I hope it's not too weird," said Elijah, scratching the back of his head. "I don't mean to bother you, but I just wanted to see how you've been?"

Riley forced a smile. "I'm good...Great, you know."

"Oh." Elijah bit his lower lip. "That's good."

"Hey!" called the elderly woman from the front of the store. "Are you going to make my drink or not?"

Riley wanted to scream at her.

Elijah glanced over his shoulder, then nervously coughed to clear his throat.

"Sorry," he said. "I can see that you're busy. I'll be working nearby for a few days, so feel free to give me a call if you'd like to meet up."

He placed a white card down on the counter.

"Okay," Riley said while trying to keep herself together. "I'll let you know."

"It was nice... to see you again." Elijah gave her a small smile before turning to leave. "Take care, Riley."

"Yeah, you too," she said back. "Good luck with your work and stuff."

"Thanks," he said with a nod.

Riley's eyes followed Elijah until he walked out the door, then disappeared from sight.

Was that really him?

Riley's mind was caught in a fog until the old woman's angry glances brought her back to reality.

"I'm going to go say something," the woman angrily muttered and got to her feet.

"Now, now," said her partner. He grabbed hold of her tracksuit to stop her. "Don't make a scene."

Riley quickly swiped Elijah's card off the counter and shoved it into her pocket, turning to fix the woman's drink.

The rest of Riley's shift passed in a blur.

Vanessa came in an hour later to help with the lunch time rush, reeking of whiskey like she'd spent another late night with a guy in the sex shed.

Riley hid herself behind the coffee machine while the other woman served customers.

Riley would occasionally pull Elijah's card out of her pocket.

It was a simple piece of cardboard with just his name, phone number and email address printed in black ink, but it was the closest she'd felt to him in years.

If she pressed it to her nose, she could almost smell him.

"Riley," said a deep voice that pierced through her daydream. "Riley," they said more loudly when she didn't respond.

"Huh?" Riley looked up to see Scott standing before her.

He was smartly dressed in a red shirt and black jeans. His beard was neatly trimmed and his long hair was tied back into a ponytail.

"Oh, hey Scott," said Riley. "Are you here for coffee?"

"I'm here to pick you up." Scott seemed confused by her dazed expression. "Don't you remember?"

"Yes...Yes... of course," said Riley. Memories of the previous day came flooding back to her. "I'll just grab my jacket."

Riley clocked out and went into the back room to grab her things.

Vanessa raised an eyebrow as she rushed past.

"Don't," said Riley.

"I wasn't going to say anything," Vanessa replied and returned her attention back to the shelf she was cleaning.

Riley quickly gathered her things.

Scott was waiting in his truck outside the store.

"Hey." Riley hopped into the passenger seat and closed the door behind her.

"Are you okay?" asked Scott. "You seem a little off."

"No," said Riley, wondering if Scott had gained the supernatural ability to sense her unease. "Why would you say that?"

"Well for starters...." Scott tapped the steering wheel. "Your sweater is inside out."

Riley looked down to see that he was right.

"Crap," she swore and pulled it over her head.

Scott laughed. "Rough shift?"

"You have no idea," Riley sighed, fixing her sweater, then putting it back on again.

Scott shifted the car into gear, then pulled out onto the main road.

"I picked up some meds for Abigail," he said. "They'll take a few days to kick in, but she seems to be taking them well."

"Is she still upset about that guy?"

"Not really. She just seems happy to be rid of that loser."

"Good for her." Riley nodded while looking out the window.

Abigail was screwed over by werewolf society, but they weren't all bad. Right?

"Elijah came into the store this morning," Riley said.

Scott hit the brakes, throwing Riley against her seat belt.

"Hey!" Riley protested. "What are you-"

"Elijah," Scott exclaimed while steering the car to a standstill by the side of the road. "As in *the* Elijah?"

"Yes," Riley said, surprised by his reaction.

"Are you okay?" Scott asked.

"Yes."

"He didn't harass you or anything?"

"No. He was just passing by."

"So he just strolled into the store?"

"Yes."

"For a coffee?"

"He didn't order anything." Riley ran her fingers over the card in her pocket. "He said that he could smell me there."

"Then what did he do?"

"He left."

"He left?"

"Yes. But he said that I can call him if I want."

Scott let out a deep sigh and ran a hand through his hair. "I'm taking you home."

He put the car into gear and pulled out onto the main road.

"It's okay," said Riley. "I want to help you with Abigail."

"Don't you think that you should just focus on yourself," Scott exclaimed. "You just met the guy who got you pregnant. You're clearly still in shock."

"I'm not in shock," Riley muttered.

"Did he do anything creepy?"

"No, he just...." Riley searched for the right words. "Seemed sad."

"Sad?"

"Yeah."

"Did he mention getting back together?"

"No." Riley shook her head. "Nothing like that."

Scott went silent. His face was solemn and he kept his eyes focused on the road.

Riley couldn't take it. She just wanted him to say something.

Why did he make her feel like she'd done something wrong?

Scott let out a sigh. "I've seen a lot of cases like yours. Sometimes werewolf guys just get caught up in the heat of the moment, but sometimes they get attached too quickly and have trouble letting go. They're terrible stalkers."

Riley rolled her eyes. She could take care of herself. She wasn't one of his little damsels in distress.

"I don't think Elijah's a stalker. We were only together for a few weeks, so he's bound to be over it by now," said Riley. "He also had other women," she bitterly added.

"Yeah. I remember you telling me about it."

"I'm sure that he's married with plenty of other children by now."

"Perhaps," Scott muttered. "That's usually how it goes."

"I think that I should tell him about Ryan."

Scott turned too quickly, throwing Riley against the seat belt.

"Scott-"

"You can't be serious," said Scott.

"Why not?" said Riley. "He's Ryan's father."

"But he's also a werewolf," said Scott.

"So?"

"There's no telling how things will go."

"But I can't not tell him. He deserves to know that he has a son."

"After everything you told me about this guy?"

"But it was his family who were mainly the problem. Elijah was always nice to me."

"But you could risk bringing these people into Ryan's life?"

"Then I'll make Elijah understand."

"It's not always as simple as that, Riley."

Riley crossed her arms. She didn't appreciate being talked down to. Scott didn't even know Elijah.

"What am I supposed to tell Ryan when he's older?" she said. "That he had an opportunity to know his father but I took that away?"

"He'll understand."

"No, he won't. Children don't think that way." Riley let out a sigh of frustration. "I don't want him to blame me."

"He won't."

"You don't know that! My parents had a shitty divorce. My mother would try and keep me from my father as a way of getting back at him. It sucked."

"But your situation is different."

"It's not that different."

"Ryan can always meet Elijah once he's older."

"But then Elijah would miss out on seeing him grow up."

"Doesn't he have other children to watch grow up?"

"Maybe.....I don't know......I don't know how their weird system works." Just thinking about it was enough to give Riley a headache. "I think that I should just tell him about Ryan and see how it goes from there. If Elijah doesn't want to be in Ryan's life, then I'll just drop it."

"I think that you should take some time to think before rushing into things."

"I'm Ryan's mother!" Riley snapped back. "Don't you think that I know what's best for my own child?"

That did it.

Scott went silent as they pulled up in front of Riley's house, restrained frustration more than evident on his face.

"Okay." He turned off the engine, then collapsed back against his seat. "Whatever you think is best, Riley."

His surrender didn't bring Riley the satisfaction that she expected.

"Thanks for the ride," she muttered and hopped out of the car. "Good luck with Abigail."

Riley shut the door behind her, then walked up to the house. She didn't bother looking back as Scott reversed down the driveway.

She was almost at the door when Ryan emerged from the bushes.

A giant smile was plastered across his little face as he dashed towards her, but his naked human body was covered in mud.

It was everywhere. Barely any skin was showing.

He smelt terrible.

"Not again," Riley moaned. She held him away at arms length to stop him from soiling her clothes. "How many times have I told you to stop rolling in animal poop!"

Ryan froze.

Riley thought that she might have gotten through to him, but then his lower lip trembled and he burst into tears, wailing in anguish as he ran off into a paddock.

Riley felt terrible.

"Ryan!" Riley called out as she chased after him. "I didn't mean it like that. Come back here!"

Ryan ignored her and continued running away.

"I'm sorry!" said Riley. "I didn't mean it like that. I'll give you a hug. I'll give you all the hugs in the world!"

Ryan continued to ignore her.

"Please, Ryan!" Riley begged.

After chasing Ryan in circles around the house, Riley finally managed to scoop him up and drag him into the bathroom.

"Look, it's a bath," Riley said with fake enthusiasm as she filled the tub with hot water. "You love baths, don't you?"

Ryan shook his head. He dashed to the door but Riley blocked his way.

"Please, Ryan," Riley begged while trying to hold him in place. "Just take a bath."

Ryan shook his head and let out a growl.

"What about some bubble bath, and toys," said Riley. "You love toys, don't you?"

That peeked Ryan's interest.

He stopped struggling and furiously pointed to a sparkly bottle of bubble bath on a high shelf.

Riley let out a sigh and pulled it down.

She tried to carefully add a small amount to the running water, but Ryan jumped and snatched it out of her hands, adding far more than necessary.

Riley was too exhausted to fight back.

Ryan jumped into the water and started splashing about, spraying water over the floor near the bath.

Riley let out a sigh and stripped her mud soaked clothes. Her hands were filthy.

She moved to the sink and attempted to wash the mud off.

"Coming through!" Trissy rushed into the bathroom carrying a mud soaked Andrea. She dumped the small girl into the bath beside Ryan.

"Andrea too?" said Riley.

"It was the twins." Trissy tugged her hair with frustration. Her shirt was also covered in mud. "It's always the twins. Those two boys are the devil reincarnated."

Riley let out a laugh.

"It's everywhere," Trissy moaned. "The kitchen, the hallway, they even started making a painting on your floor."

The laughter instantly died in Riley's throat.

She looked to her son who was merrily spraying water at Andrea.

"Like I don't already have enough to deal with." Trissy took a handful of shampoo and began to massage it through Andrea's hair. "Andrea is still waking up at night, and Tabitha won't sleep in her own bed. I barely slept at all last night."

"Must be hard," said Riley. Listening to Trissy made her grateful that she only had one child.

"You have no idea." Trissy finished washing Andrea's hair, then started on Ryan's. "Mia's also being difficult. I had to ask her three times to go hang out the laundry."

"Oh, I thought she was the helpful one."

"*Was*," said Trissy. "But then she hit puberty."

Riley nodded. She finished washing her hands, then dried them with a towel.

"My sister doesn't have any kids," said Trissy. "She keeps sending me pictures of her garden. I can't imagine having the free time to take pictures of grass and insects."

"Truck!" said Andrea with a smile as she held up a bath toy.

"Yes, that's a lovely car," said Trissy without looking.

"Do you ever wish that you didn't have children?" asked Riley.

"It's too late for that," said Trissy. She picked up a small bucket and poured water over Ryan's head. "They're all here and nobody else is going to raise them."

Riley nodded.

"Why do you ask," said Trissy. "Do you regret..." she pointed down at Ryan.

"No..I.." Riley bit her lip as she tried to sort out her own thoughts. "Just worry about his future."

"Well, that's what having kids is like," said Trissy. "It's just worrying.. Worrying and more worrying."

"Oh," said Riley, that didn't make her feel any better. "Do you think things would be easier if their father was around?"

"Hell no, he was the biggest baby of them all."

"I'm a baby!" Andrea declared while splashing water.

"Yes, you are." Trissy lathered soap on her small daughter. "I should have just walked out on that loser sooner. I wasted years of my life hoping that he was gonna change and he never did."

"I see," said Riley. She'd heard plenty of stories about Trissy's werewolf ex-husband. "Have you ever thought of co-parenting?"

Trissy stopped washing her daughter and stared at Riley like she was insane.

"It could work...." Riley lost her confidence as Trissy continued to stare. "Maybe......"

"Mom!" called Trissy's son Jacob from the kitchen. "I tried hosing down the twins but they keep running away."

"Motherfudger," Trissy swore and got to her feet.

Trissy pulled Andrea out of the bath and quickly wrapped her in a towel, carrying her out of the bathroom.

"Boys!" Trissy yelled at the top of her lungs. "Get back here now!" She stomped down the hall and out of sight.

Riley pulled out a fresh towel and showed it to Ryan.

"Come on, little man," she said gently. "Time to get out."

Ryan shook his head and continued to play.

Riley sighed and sat down on the bathroom floor. She thought of going to her room to start cleaning, but she needed to keep an eye on Ryan to make sure that he didn't drown.

Watching him smash two trucks together wasn't the most exciting thing she'd ever seen, but at least Ryan looked happy.

Was it really a good idea to mess with that?

What if Scott was right? What if things were better if they had nothing to do with Elijah?

Riley had heard enough horror stories about werewolves to last a lifetime.

They mindlessly took orders from their elders like a bunch of little drones, fucking themselves senseless and throwing their weight around like self entitled arseholes.

When Ryan was born Riley decided that it was better not to seek out Elijah. She was still raw from giving birth and didn't feel comfortable seeing him again.

She was afraid that he'd try to take control of her life and drag them back to the academy.

But seeing Elijah again in the coffee shop made her think differently.

Riley was starting to wonder if she had been wrong.

Ryan was a werewolf since birth and there was still so much that she didn't understand. Was it really okay to deny him the chance to know his werewolf father?

Riley's own relationship with her parents was terrible.

As a child, she was selfishly used as a bargaining chip between them, then practically forgotten once they both remarried.

She didn't want to do the same to Ryan.

Riley spent the rest of the evening looking after Ryan. She fed him dinner then put him to bed. It took Riley an hour of pretending to be asleep until he eventually dozed off beside her.

Riley moved Ryan's sleeping body to his own bed, then slipped outside.

The properties surrounding them were full of retirees, so all was silent except for the cries of children playing inside and the rustling of wind blowing through the long grass.

The hills around the farm were blanketed in darkness. Not even the moon could illuminate the pitch black forest.

Riley shivered in the evening chill.

She used the light from the verandah to read the number on Elijah's card, twirling it between her fingers as she struggled to come to a decision.

Doing nothing was the easiest option. She and Ryan would live out their days far from werewolf society. She'd give Ryan some vague details about his father, then allow her son to try and find Elijah once he was older, and only if he wanted to.

But there was no guarantee that Elijah would still be around by then.

Elijah was still young but he wasn't immortal. What if he got sick and died? What if Elijah became too busy with his new family to have any time for Ryan?

Was it really fair to force her son to grow up without a father?

With a deep breath, Riley gathered her courage and dialed Elijah's number.

Just speaking to him couldn't hurt, right?

She pressed the call button.

It rang several times before Elijah answered.

"Hello?" he said softly.

His deep voice struck deep within her core.

Somewhere within Riley, her inner wolf stirred.

"Hey." Riley tried to hide her anxiety and sound as natural as possible. "It's me."

"Riley?"

"Yeah."

There was silence for a moment, then the sound of faint shuffling.

"It's good to hear from you," Elijah said. "I'm glad that you called."

How glad? Riley wondered to herself. *Does he really mean it?*

Riley nervously paced back and forth before the house.

"I just wanted to ask if you're still interested in catching up," she said. "If you're busy, then I completely understa-"

"No, no, it's okay," said Elijah. "I have some free time over the next few days."

"Great." Riley unconsciously forced a smile. "Are you free tomorrow evening?"

"Yes. Where do you want to meet?"

Riley paused.

She didn't feel comfortable inviting him straight to her home. She wanted to at least talk to him first before introducing him to Ryan.

"How about the cafe where I work?" she said. "I finish at five, so I can talk to you then."

"Sounds good," said Elijah.

"Okay." Riley struggled to think of what else to say. "See you tomorrow."

"See you then."

"Night."

"Goodnight, Riley," Elijah said softly before Riley quickly hung up.

She'd done it.

She'd arranged a meeting with Elijah.

Riley looked away from her phone and towards the dark hills, hoping that she'd made the right choice.

CHAPTER THREE

Riley spent the next morning failing to homeschool Ryan.

He liked listening to songs and watching videos on her phone, but it was impossible to make him sit down and concentrate.

He'd soon become distracted and walk away, transforming into a wolf to wreak havoc around the house if she didn't let him outside.

"And then the little turtle went over to Mr. Rabbit's house," said Riley as she half-heartedly showed Ryan a bright picture book. "But Mr. Rabbit was still-"

She was cut off by Ryan lunging forward to turn the pages.

"Come on, Ryan," Riley moaned. "Just let me tell the story."

Ryan ripped the book from her hand, rapidly flipping through the pages as he looked at the pictures.

Riley was too exhausted to fight with him.

"What was Mr. Rabbit doing?" asked Trissy's daughter Andrea.

She was sitting at the children's table, coloring book and crayons neatly laid out before her. She was wearing a bright pink dress and her short blonde hair was tied back into two adorable pigtails.

Beside her sat one of the twins. He held several pencils in his fist as he rubbed them against the paper until they made a hole.

"He was doing a poo!" the small boy cried out.

Andrea and her brother burst into laughter, cackling at the top of their lungs.

Despite being younger than Ryan, Andrea had no trouble talking. She was picking up new words every day and would often ask questions about the world around her. She also didn't throw tantrums over having to wear clothes.

Watching her progress only made Riley feel worse about Ryan.

What if there was something developmentally wrong with her son?

Ryan went and stood before the door, furiously pointing at the lock like he wanted to go out.

Riley let out a sigh and went to unlock the door.

Ryan dashed outside the moment that it cracked open, transforming into a black wolf and disappearing behind the trees.

Riley closed the door and went back into the kitchen, cleaning up all the books and pencils that Ryan had thrown on the floor.

"You're wasting your time," said Trissy as she walked past carrying a large basket of fresh laundry. "The wolf is strong in that one."

"Were your kids like this?"

"No," she said. "But their father would have bit their head off if they didn't do as they were told."

Riley's heart sank.

It was just another reminder that she couldn't control her own child.

"Just give it another year or two," said Trissy when she noticed the devastation on Riley's face. "Werewolf children develop differently than humans."

"Yeah," Riley muttered. "Maybe." She arranged all the picture books into a neat pile. "Do you think that Ryan's father would know what to do?"

"Hell if I know," huffed Trissy. "I've never met him."

Riley realized how stupid her question sounded.

"Didn't you say that he was an arrogant werewolf fascist with seven wives?" asked Trissy.

Riley felt her face turning red. "I don't think I would have said that."

"No. I think you did," said Trissy. "I also remember you saying that he was a sex-crazed blonde supremacist with bitchy parents."

"Well...." Riley looked to Andrea and her brother to see the two small children watching them with rapt attention. "I was a little angry after we broke up."

"Just a little?"

"Okay. Maybe a lot," Riley sighed.

She finished picking up the pencils, then slipped them back into their tin.

Riley thought of asking Trissy her opinion on meeting Elijah, then decided against it.

Trissy was trapped with an oppressive group of werewolves for years. She would certainly advise Riley against meeting Elijah.

"I have some stuff that I need to do after work today," said Riley. "I might be home a little later than normal."

"Just as long as it's not too late," said Trissy. "In case you haven't forgotten, I still have another seven children that I'm trying to keep alive."

Six, Riley almost corrected. Trissy's oldest son had refused to leave with her.

"Am I alive, Mummy?" asked Andrea from her table.

"Of course, Sweetie," Trissy said with a small smile.

"It shouldn't be too late," said Riley. "I'll let you know if anything comes up."

"All right," said Trissy. "And let me know if Vanessa talks about bringing any men back. Jacob went into the shed to get a shovel this morning, only to find....." She glanced over to her children. "One of her *friends* naked and handcuffed to the wall."

"Oh," said Riley.

"That's one conversation with my son that I never want to have again."

Trissy pushed open the door and carried the laundry out to the clothes line.

"I'll let you know if she says anything!" Riley called out.

"What does *chained* mean?" Andrea asked.

"Well..." Riley tried to think of an appropriate answer.

"It means poo!" her brother replied, sending the two children into a fit of giggles again.

Riley watched them fall to the floor as they continued their exaggerated laughter like it was a new game.

Sometimes she was glad that Ryan didn't talk.

Riley's shift at the cafe seemed to drag on forever. Weekday afternoons were always quiet. She spent most of the time cleaning down counters and arranging cupboards.

Vanessa lingered more than usual, occasionally looking in Riley's direction.

Riley suspected that Scott had told her about Elijah.

Scott and Vanessa once dated, even though Riley had a hard time imagining Scott being into Vanessa's weird kinks.

Let her stay, Riley thought as Vanessa helped herself to a fifth cup of coffee. *At least there'll be someone around in case something goes wrong.*

Once four-thirty arrived, Riley's anxiety spiked.

Maybe she couldn't do it?

Perhaps it was a terrible idea?

Was it too late to cancel?

Riley wanted to go home and hide, but Elijah knew where she worked. He'd find her eventually.

She was fucked.

Vanessa appeared before Riley, carrying her coat and keys.

"I'm heading out," said Vanessa. "Some guy wants to meet me down at the beach. Are you okay closing up by yourself?"

"Yep." Riley tried not to let her anxiety show. "Not a problem."

"Okay," said Vanessa hesitantly like she could see through Riley's act. "Let me know if anything comes up."

"Will do," Riley nervously laughed. "Enjoy your night."

"Oh, I will," Vanessa said with a wink. She put on her coat and walked out the door, leaving Riley alone in the store.

Riley grabbed a broom and started sweeping the floor.

Maybe she and Ryan could run away? They could build a cabin in the wilderness and Ryan could run free. They could spend the rest of their lives living as loners in the forest.

The bell above the door jingled.

Riley looked up to see Elijah enter.

He looked out of place amongst her new life. His crisp outfit clashed with the worn antique furniture surrounding them.

"Riley," he said with a small nod.

Riley's heart skipped a beat.

Her name sounded good when it rolled off his tongue.

Memories of what else he used to do with that tongue floated to the surface of her mind.

"Hey." Riley hastily propped the broom against the wall and wiped her hands on her apron. "Can I get you anything? A coffee....or tea.....maybe a bagel?"

Elijah slipped his jacket off his shoulders, unveiling a dark blue sweater which neatly fit his broad chest. "A coffee would be great, thanks."

"Sure, coming right up."

Riley hid herself behind the coffee machine as she made his drink, trying to avoid looking at him as much as possible.

She could still remember what he looked like under that sweater.

Stop it, she told herself. *You shouldn't be thinking about that.*

"How do you prefer your coffee?" Riley asked. "Latte, cappuccino....flat white?"

Elijah took a seat on one of the couches at the front of the store. "Whichever is fine."

"Okay," said Riley. "Latte it is."

She finished preparing his drink and brought it out to Elijah, placing it down on the small table before them.

Riley took a seat on the sofa opposite him. She was surprised when he continued to stare at her.

"Aren't you having anything?" Elijah asked.

Crap, Riley thought as she felt a stab of embarrassment.

She was too busy thinking about Elijah to get her own drink.

"Oh, I'm not really that thirsty," she said with a wave of her hand. "Go ahead."

"Okay." Elijah reached forward to hesitantly take a sip.

Riley gazed down at his elegant hands and well kept nails.

She never expected to be sitting face to face with Elijah again.

But things were different now.

She wasn't a stupid teenager anymore.

She wouldn't allow herself to be so easily controlled by her hormones again.

"So..." Riley tried to think of a way to break the silence. "What have you been up to these past five years?"

"Not much," said Elijah. "I moved back home and started helping my grandfather."

"Like looking after him?"

"No," Elijah laughed, tension leaving his shoulders. "He can still look after himself. He just wants me to help him with work."

"Oh. What sort of work does he do?"

"Things for the council. Mostly meetings with elders and traveling to other clans."

"Is that what brought you out here?"

"Yeah." He took a sip of coffee. "You could say that."

Elijah's gaze seemed to pierce straight through her.

Riley looked down at her lap. She wished that she had her own beverage to keep her hands busy.

"What about you?" Elijah asked. "Have you been out here the whole time?"

"I went back home for a bit, but...." She wasn't sure how to explain it without mentioning Ryan. "I decided to come live out here with some friends."

"Must be some friends."

"Yeah...they're all very...unique."

"Do you like working here?" He gestured to the space around them.

"It's alright," Riley said. "It's okay for now, but I hope to go back to school later."

Elijah nodded while taking another sip of coffee.

Riley's hands gripped her apron. She wanted to talk about Ryan, but once she told him there was no going back.

"How's Latavia?" Riley blurted out.

Shit, she thought. *That was way too direct.*

Elijah didn't look bothered. He calmly placed his mug down on the saucer. "I wouldn't know. We haven't spoken in months."

"Oh."

"The elders decided every thing for us. We were never a good couple."

"I'm sorry to hear that." Riley said even though part of her was glad. She didn't want to see that stuck up bitch again.

"It's okay," said Elijah. "Maybe things are better this way."

"Yeah," Riley said. "Perhaps."

"What about you?" Elijah asked. "Are you dating anyone?"

"No, no," Riley laughed. "I'm not really into dating. I'm a bit of a lone wolf." She paused when she realized how ridiculous that sounded. "Excuse the pun."

"You're excused," Elijah slyly smiled.

Silence grew between them as Riley ran out of small talk ideas.

She tapped her fingers on her knee, gathering her courage.

It would be cowardly to back down.

She needed to tell him.

"Elijah..." It took immense effort to force the words out of her mouth. "There's something that I need to tell you."

"What is it?" he asked softly like he could sense her distress.

"I had a son." Her gaze fell to the floor, too afraid to see his reaction. "Your son."

Elijah was silent as he processed her words. "Are you sure?"

"Yes, I didn't sleep with anyone else."

Riley's face felt numb as her lower lip trembled.

The stress from the past five years came crashing down.

She was powerless to stop the tears that flowed forth.

Don't cry, you idiot, Riley told herself, but it was already too late.

Elijah quickly put down his mug. He got up to sit beside her on the sofa, wrapping one arm around her back.

"Hey," he said gently. "There's no need to cry. Children are a blessing."

Riley couldn't help but inhale his scent.

It was duller because of her medication, but it was still familiar and comforting.

Him....

It felt like they had never been apart.

Riley buried her face against Elijah's sweater.

"I know," she sobbed. "I know."

Elijah was silent as he let Riley cry it out, occasionally patting her back.

Was he always this gentle?

"Tell me about him?" Elijah asked softly.

"His name is Ryan." Riley struggled to pull herself away. She picked up a discarded napkin to wipe her face. "He kinda looks like you, and he has so much energy."

"Is he a werewolf?"

"Yes."

"That's good."

"Really?" It had only caused Riley stress until that moment.

"Of course," said Elijah like it was the most natural thing in the world. "He's been blessed."

Of course Elijah would think that, thought Riley. *He's spent his entire life surrounded by werewolves.*

Children like Ryan were nothing strange where Elijah was from.

"Would you like to meet him?" Riley asked.

"Of course." Elijah's mouth broke out into a grin. "My car is parked out front."

"Now?" Riley exclaimed.

"Why not?" Elijah's smile disappeared as he noticed her shocked expression. "Or not..."

"No, it's fine." Riley stood to her feet and started clearing the table. "We can go now."

If Elijah was going to meet Ryan eventually, then it might as well be now. Riley picked up Elijah's empty cup. "Just give me a moment to close up."

CHAPTER FOUR

Trissy was outside watching her children play as Elijah's car rolled up the gravel driveway. There were bags under her eyes and she was clearly exhausted.

Andrea had her tiny arms wrapped around Trissy's neck, loudly sobbing like she had skipped her nap again.

Trissy raked her critical gaze over Elijah's toned body as they emerged from the car.

"You're gonna have to do it in the shed," Trissy said.

Riley wanted to roll over and die.

"We're not going to be doing *that*," she muttered, face turning red.

Elijah looked between them. "Doing what?"

"Nothing," Riley snapped back. "The house is pretty crowded so.... sometimes we just entertain guests in the shed."

"In a shed?"

"It's a very lovely shed," Riley said even though it was a lie. There was nothing in there except old garden tools, broken furniture, and a crappy bed that was stained from Vanessa's sexcapades.

Trissy's son Jacob transformed into a human boy, spitting a frisbee out of his mouth.

"Is he going to come live with us?" Jacob enthusiastically asked.

"Of course not," Trissy snapped. "She can move in with him."

"Where's Ryan?" Riley quickly asked. Trissy was a nightmare to deal with when she was exhausted, and Riley needed to get away before the children's questions got any worse.

"Last time I saw him he was playing in the sandbox," Trissy said.

"Okay. Thanks." Riley grabbed Elijah's sleeve, quickly tugging him away.

"Sorry about that," she muttered. "Trissy's pretty snappy when she's had a rough day."

"Is she one of the friends you were talking about?"

"Kinda...in a way." Riley didn't even know Trissy until after Ryan was born. "We mostly just use each other for childcare."

Elijah gazed around at the run down house and overgrown fields. "Is this really where you live? It seems kinda old."

"Yeah, but the rent's cheap and it has tons of space."

"Is that a goat?"

"Yep, great for free milk."

Riley dragged Elijah to the back of the house.

Ryan was sitting alone in the sand box.

He was pushing a plastic truck around several buckets, making exaggerated beeping noises.

"Ryan!" Riley called out.

He looked up and smiled when he saw Riley, but looked hesitantly at Elijah, like he didn't know what to think.

Usually he would immediately run over to greet her, but instead he stayed put.

"Hey, Ryan," Riley said gently as they approached him. "There's someone that I want you to meet." She pointed to Elijah. "This is your father."

Riley wasn't sure what she expected. Maybe some dramatic heartfelt reunion like a daytime Christian movie.

But instead Ryan just shrugged his shoulders and went back to playing, pushing his truck over a mountain of sand like they weren't even there.

"Ryan," Riley said more hopefully. "Don't you want to say *hello*."

Ryan shook his head.

Elijah took a step closer and lowered himself to Ryan's level. He took one of the trucks in the sandbox and attempted to place it beside Ryan's, but Ryan completely freaked out.

The small boy jumped to his feet and dashed behind Riley, clinging to her leg.

It was worse than she expected.

"I'm sorry," Riley apologized. "He's very shy. It usually takes him a while to warm up to people."

"It's okay," Elijah said calmly, but the disappointment was obvious on his face. "I know what kids can be like."

"Ryan." Riley tried to pry her son from her leg but he refused to let go. "Why don't you show Elijah your trucks?"

Ryan shook his head.

"Ryan," Riley begged, but her son refused to budge. "Just say *hello*."

"How about I come back tomorrow?" said Elijah. "It's getting late, so he must be tired."

"I'm sorry," said Riley. "He's usually much more energetic."

"It's okay," said Elijah. "You don't need to apologize."

"He likes the beach down the road," said Riley. "Maybe we could go there tomorrow morning... if it's not too much trouble."

"No, it's no trouble at all. I have to make some calls in the morning, but I can come after that."

"Great." Riley smiled. "Did you hear that Ryan?" She patted her son on the back. "We're going to the beach tomorrow."

Ryan didn't let go of her leg, but for one short moment, there was a small smile on his face.

Riley felt hope.

"Well....I should get going." Elijah took a step back. "We can talk more tomorrow."

"Okay," said Riley. "Sounds good."

She walked with Elijah back to his car. The new white hybrid was smeared with dirt from the drive-in.

Jacob and his sister Tabitha had their faces pressed to the window, gazing in to admire the decor.

"Okay, time to back off kids," said Riley. "Elijah needs to go home."

Tabitha curiously gazed up at Elijah. "Is he a maybe man?"

"A maybe man?" asked Riley.

"Vanessa calls them maybe mans," said Tabitha. "Cause one of them maybe gets to be her boyfriend."

Riley cringed. "No, Tabitha."

"Who's Vanessa?" asked Elijah.

"Just another woman who lives here," Riley nervously laughed while nudging Jacob and Tabitha back from the car.

"How many people live here?" Elijah asked.

"Ten," said Jacob.

"Thirteen," said his sister.

"Come on guys." Riley threw her arms around the children's shoulders and started leading them back to the house. "Don't you guys have chores to do?"

"There's ten," Jacob snapped back at Tabitha.

"Thirteen!" Tabitha yelled back.

"Ten!"

"What about Wilfred and Sunny!" Tabitha whined.

"Those are fucking chickens, Tabitha!"

"Language!" Trissy yelled out from across the yard.

"I'll see you tomorrow!" Riley called out to Elijah.

Elijah watched her with a perplexed expression before hopping into his car. He gave Riley one last wave before reversing back down the driveway.

Trissy walked over to scold Jacob, but he immediately fled, transforming back into a wolf and dashing into the forest.

Trissy let out an exasperated sigh and looked to where Elijah's car had been parked moments earlier.

"George was like that too," said Trissy. "Always showing up with the sad puppy eyes to try and make me take him back."

"It's not like that," Riley said.

She didn't like Trisssy lumping Elijah in with her crazy ex-husband.

"Whatever you say," Trissy muttered and returned to her other children.

"Come on." Riley took hold of Tabitha's shoulders and led her inside. "Let's get started on dinner."

CHAPTER FIVE

The house was silent and cloaked in darkness.

No snoring, no crying, no Trissy yelling at a child to get back to bed.

It was abnormal.

Riley stirred and looked over to Ryan's bed to see that it was empty. The sheets were gone like he'd never existed.

It didn't scare her like it should have.

Elijah stood in the doorway, lethargically leaning against the frame while silently watching her.

His upper half was bare, wide chest proudly on display. His hair was ruffled and his blue eyes glimmered in the darkness.

He silently walked towards her like he was floating on air, slipping himself under her sheets.

Excitement pounded in Riley's chest as his warm naked body pressed against hers. His smooth chest felt pleasant against her erect breasts, and she could feel his hard cock against her inner thighs.

Elijah slipped himself inside her wet heat with a sigh, slowly thrusting back and forth in a perfect rhythm.

Riley wrapped her arms and legs around his body to bring him closer, enjoying the smooth slide of his cock.

It was nice.

This was what she missed most.

The warm intimacy of being joined together. To feel his heart beat against her own.

There was no need to fight it.

Riley moaned and shifted her hips to get more friction. Addictive pleasure began to build deep within her core.

She needed it.

She wanted everything.

Riley was startled awake by Ryan crying.

She opened her eyes to see him standing over her bed, rubbing his face as his small shoulders shook.

"Hey," Riley said sleepily. "Did you have a nightmare?"

Ryan nodded.

Riley pulled back her blanket and shuffled to the other side of the bed.

Ryan slid in beside her, transforming back into a wolf and curling up against her side. His breathing gradually evened out as he drifted off to sleep.

Riley watched the shadows dance across the wall.

She could hear Jacob muttering in his sleep in the next room, and Vanessa's laughter from the shed outside.

It had just been another dream.

After seeing Elijah again, it was easy to think that it was real. She could still feel his warm hands against her skin.

Why did her body refuse to get over him? Was it because he was the last guy that she ever slept with?

Was it because he was the only one who made her feel good?

Riley rolled onto her side and tried to get back to sleep, but it was impossible. Her body felt hot and bothered from the dream. It was uncomfortable to leave herself hanging.

She slipped out of bed and went to the bathroom, switching on the bright fluorescent light and locking the door behind her.

Riley stripped her clothes and turned on the shower, stepping under the spray.

The warm water felt heavenly against her skin.

The space between Riley's legs was already wet, caused by the graphic sex dream. It was easy to slide one hand between her thighs to stimulate her aching clit.

Riley moaned with relief, bracing herself against the shower wall as she rubbed back and forth.

Yes. This was what her body wanted.

She didn't need a man.

All she needed was her own hand if she wanted to get herself off.

Pleasure grew in her center, stronger and more consuming than when she usually touched herself.

She could still picture Elijah behind her closed eyes.

His naked body as he stalked towards her.

The feeling of his cock deep inside her.

The way that his dark sweater sat on his toned upper body in the coffee shop.

Riley bit down on her hand to muffle her moans.

She stopped holding back and just let go, quickly rubbing herself to the point of no return.

Pure happiness washed over her, then her body peaked and crashed, trembling and shaking as she worked herself through the orgasm.

Fuck, it felt good.

All her worries and concerns evaporated away.

Riley leant back against the shower wall to catch her breath, relaxing into the post orgasm high.

She washed her body, then turned off the water, stepping out of the shower then wrapping herself in a towel.

She opened the medicine cabinet above the sink and took out her bottle of pills.

Riley swallowed three of them dry.

CHAPTER SIX

The next morning, Riley thought of calling off the meeting with Elijah, but she didn't want to explain why.

Sorry, I had a vivid sex dream about you, then used it to wank myself stupid, didn't sound like a good excuse.

At least Ryan would be there.

Riley didn't have to worry about her vagina running wild as long as her son was around.

Riley got dressed and ready for the day. She brushed her teeth while anxiously staring at her phone, wondering if Elijah would call or text before showing up.

Maybe he wouldn't come? Maybe one afternoon with her was enough to send him running back to the mountains?

Riley jumped when she noticed Vanessa's reflection in the mirror.

Vanessa was standing behind Riley, leaning against the door frame with her arms crossed over her chest. She was wearing a tight black t-shirt and small denim shorts.

"Geez." Riley spat into the sink. "Don't scare me like that."

A smile crept across Vanessa's face. "You didn't tell me that your ex was hot."

"He's not really an ex," Riley muttered. "I don't think that we were together long enough to count as dating."

"Then what do you call it?"

"More like a....summer fling... ish."

Vanessa nodded. She walked into the bathroom and started picking up the discarded towels. "Given all the bitching and moaning you made about him, I thought that he'd be uglier."

"I never said that he was ugly."

"But you never said that he was hot either. Why did you break up?"

"His mother was a bitch."

Vanessa huffed. "All mothers are bitches."

"His fiance was also a bitch."

"Ouch. Weren't keen on being the third wheel?"

"No." Riley pulled a bottle of make-up from the cupboard and began applying it to her face. "I'm pretty sure that there was a fourth and fifth wheel rolling around somewhere too."

"Yeah, typical. That's just how werewolves tend to roll." Vanessa placed the towels into the laundry basket. "That's why I gave up on relationships long ago."

Riley nodded. She doubted that Vanessa would ever let herself get tied down, even if she wasn't a werewolf.

Riley paused while screwing the lid back onto her foundation. "Hey.... How do you even know what Elijah looks like?"

She had no memory of Vanessa and Elijah being in the same place at once.

"Because he's outside right now," said Vanessa.

"Shit." Riley threw the rest of her make-up back into her bag. "How long's he been there?"

"Not long. Jacob's interrogating him now as we speak."

Riley cracked open the window and peered outside.

Elijah was standing before his car with Jacob curiously looking up at him.

Trissy's oldest daughter Mia was off her phone for once. She stood behind Jacob, letting out the occasional giggle as she stared up at Elijah.

"Why are you so pale?" asked Jacob. "Are you a vampire?"

Riley quickly pulled her head back inside.

"Do I look okay?" Riley asked Vanessa. "Should I put on some lipstick? But that might make me look like I'm trying too hard."

"You look fine." Vanessa smiled.

"Really?" Riley looked down at the simple T-shirt and long skirt that she was wearing. "Maybe I should change into something else."

"Are you trying to get into his pants?"

"No."

"Then why does it matter?"

Vanessa had a good point.

"It would be cool if Ryan had a little brother," echoed Jacob's voice from outside.

Riley quickly scooped up her things and dumped them into the cupboard under the sink. She returned the child lock, then rushed out of the room.

"Good luck!" Vanessa yelled after her.

Ryan was watching T.V. He was immersed in a cartoon about dogs, dancing with Andrea to the theme song as she sang it at the top of her lungs.

By the time Riley got him ready and out of the house. Trissy's children had already dragged Elijah into the garden, giving him a tour of the flowers and vegetables.

"These are my potatoes," said Jacob, pointing to an overgrown vegetable garden with utmost seriousness. "We'd all starve to death if it weren't for me."

Elijah looked like he needed saving.

"Hey," Elijah smiled with relief when Riley approached him. "Are you ready?"

"Yes." Riley smiled. "Let's get out of here."

The beach was a small cove situated between two hills. It was a short walk from the farm, and far from town, so only the people who lived nearby ever used it.

Riley and Ryan usually spent hours there without anyone showing up.

Ryan kept his distance from Elijah for most of the walk. He trailed behind them in wolf form, but seemed less hesitant than the previous day.

Elijah tried to greet him, but Ryan hid straight behind Riley.

Riley's heart sank.

How could she get him to open up?

Elijah rustled around in his pocket. He pulled out what looked like a small candy wrapped in silver paper.

He offered it to Ryan.

Their son eyed it curiously.

"What's that?" Riley asked.

"It's dried meat," said Elijah. "It's pretty popular with werewolf kids."

Ryan paused and transformed back into his human form. He snatched it out of Elijah's hand, then unwrapped the paper and popped the piece of dried meat into his mouth, happily chewing it.

Riley smiled.

It was a start.

They followed a narrow path through the forest and soon emerged at the beach. The overcast sky made the ocean appear grey.

Riley plonked her bag down on the coarse sand. She rolled out a blanket for them to sit on.

"No swimming today," Riley said to Ryan. She reached into her bag to pull out some toys. "The water is cold so-"

There was a loud splashing as Ryan dove straight into the waves.

Riley groaned and turned around.

Ryan happily frolicked in the water in wolf form, bouncing through the waves like an overeager puppy.

If Riley forced him out, it would only lead to a meltdown.

Elijah laughed. "Kids, huh?"

"He never listens to me," Riley huffed. "He's gonna catch a cold."

"It's okay," said Elijah. "He's a werewolf. A little cold water won't hurt him."

"Maybe. But it's still dangerous. And he's always trying to go out deeper."

"I'll watch him," Elijah slipped off his jacket, followed by his shirt, jeans, and underwear.

It was the first time that Riley had seen Elijah naked in years, but his strong body didn't differ much from her steamy dreams.

Riley quickly forced herself to look away before he could catch her staring.

She'd forgotten how casual werewolves were about nudity.

Elijah's bones cracked as he transformed.

His body shrunk and spouted fur, until his form shifted into a large white wolf. His glossy fur was pale like the moon, and his blue eyes retained their alluring gaze.

Seeing Elijah's wolf form stirred something within Riley.

She shifted uncomfortably as she shoved the strange feeling back into the depths of her mind.

Elijah dashed into the water and joined Ryan in the waves, interacting with him in ways that Riley wouldn't dare.

Ryan looked thrilled to have an adult wolf giving him attention, running in circles like he was trying to play tag.

Riley hadn't transformed into a wolf in years.

The medication worked well when she was in human form, but if she changed into a wolf, it was impossible to block out all the strange urges.

She wasn't sure what her inner wolf would do if she let it roam free.

She had long decided that it would be better to live out the rest of her life as a human.

Riley drew patterns in the sand by her feet, glancing up at Ryan and Elijah every now and again to see what they were doing.

All of Ryan's shyness seemed to have disappeared. He happily followed Elijah as they paddled through the water.

After an hour of playing, Elijah emerged, transforming back into a human as he walked across the sand.

His soaked hair was plastered to his face as droplets of water rolled down his smooth chest.

He strode towards her without an ounce of shame.

Fuuuuuuuck! Riley thought as blood rushed to her face.

She quickly looked down at her feet, trying to get her breathing under control while thinking unsexy thoughts.

Pregnancy, childbirth, sleepless nights, Riley thought as she tried to get her vagina under control. *He's only walking around butt naked because werewolves have no shame.*

Elijah took a towel from her bag to pat himself dry.

If Riley just turned her head, she'd definitely get a clear view of his balls.

This couldn't go on any longer.

"We should start heading back soon." The words quickly rolled off her tongue. "I have to get ready for work."

Elijah dried his hair. "At the coffee shop?"

"Yes, the coffee shop."

Riley had a shift at two, so it wasn't a complete lie.

"Okay." Elijah picked up his shirt from the sand. "Let's head back."

Riley managed to coax Ryan out of the water by showing him kids videos on her phone.

The annoying melodies and bright animation drove her insane, but they were like crack to small children.

Ryan emerged out of the water like a moth to a flashlight, following behind Riley as she kept the phone just out of his reach.

Elijah was silent during the walk back. He occasionally glanced at her and Ryan.

Riley assumed that he was feeling down because he'd soon have to leave. Maybe he had to leave town and wouldn't be back for a while.

What if he became too caught up in his new life to visit them again?

Riley wanted to help him build a relationship with their son, but she didn't know how. She'd never had a decent male role model growing up, and her own father stopped reaching out once he married his second wife.

What if the same thing happened to Ryan?

Their son immediately rushed off to play in the sandpit as soon as they got home.

Riley walked closer to see Scott and Abigail checking out Jacob's vegetable garden.

Abigail was using one of Riley's old shirts as a dress. It only came down to the top of her thighs, but Riley was too busy mulling over Elijah to notice the young woman's questionable fashion choices.

"Hey! It's great to see you again!" Abigail rushed towards Riley with a bright smile, engulfing Riley in a tight hug.

"Right back at you," Riley wheezed, half-heartedly patting her back. She was unaware that they were now friends.

"Hey." Scott walked over, eyeing Elijah hesitantly. "I brought Abigail over to meet Trissy and the kids."

"Andrea is so cute!" Abigail squealed. "I wonder if I'll have any werewolf kids!"

"You might have to get with a werewolf for that to happen," said Riley. She'd heard that the chances were a lot lower for people who had been born human.

Abigail pulled away from Riley. Her eyes gazed over Elijah, mouth curving up into a shy smile.

"Who's your friend?" she whispered to Riley.

"Oh, that's just Ryan's father," said Riley.

"Your husband?"

"No, no," Riley hissed back. "It was only a one time thing."

"So you're not together at all?"

"God no," Riley quickly replied. "Just trying out the co-parenting thing."

"Is that so?" Abigail's mouth curved up into a sly smile.

Before Riley could stop her, she pranced over to Elijah. Swaying her hips like she wasn't even bothering to be subtle.

"Why hello there," Abigail said playfully and held out one hand. "I don't think we've met."

Elijah stared at her blankly like he wasn't fooled by her flirting.

"There's no need to be shy," Abigail laughed and moved in closer. "I'm Abigail. What's your name?"

She reached out to place a hand on Elijah's bicep, but Elijah's hand shot out to grab her wrist.

"Don't touch me," he growled then knocked her hand away.

Abigail looked shocked.

She took a step back, anxiously rubbing her wrist.

"I'm sorry." Abigail's voice was strained. She blinked several times as she tried to hold back tears. "I don't know what came over me."

Scott stepped forward and placed a comforting arm around her shoulder. "It's okay. Why don't you go take a break inside."

"Yeah," said Abigail. "That sounds like a good idea."

She slipped out of Scott's grip and walked towards the house. Pace slow and lethargic as though caught in a daze.

Scott looked directly at Elijah. "Shouldn't you be heading off too?" he said firmly.

Seriously? Riley thought. *Could he be any colder?*

Elijah didn't look pleased either.

Riley could tell that he wanted to say something, but he took one look at Riley, then ground his teeth.

"Yeah. I was just about to leave." He reached forward to give Riley a brief hug. "I'll catch you later."

Riley's body tingled from his touch. Her head felt foggy.

"Yeah, later," she mumbled.

Elijah waved goodbye to Ryan who was fully immersed in the sandpit. "See you later buddy."

Ryan gave him a small wave back without looking away from his toys.

Scott didn't back down. He remained silent and stoic until Elijah got back into his car and disappeared down the road.

"What was that?" Riley snapped at Scott. "Why were you so rude? You don't even know him."

"Oh, I think I know enough," said Scott.

"He was only defending himself from Abigail's creepy flirting."

"She's a new werewolf, Riley. She's not in control of her own actions."

"She seemed completely in control to me."

"I thought that you of all people would understand what it's like to lose control in front of the opposite sex."

"What's that supposed to mean," Riley snapped.

Scott fell silent. He glanced to the ground and rubbed his jaw.

"Look...I.." He grabbed Riley's elbow, pulling her further into the field and out of Ryan's earshot. "Don't you think this is all moving a little fast? You only ran into him two days ago, but he's already hanging out with Ryan?"

"He's Ryan's father. He deserves a chance to get to know his own son."

"But what's he even doing in East Cove?"

"He has work."

"What sort of work?"

"I don't know. Just work."

"How long is he here for?"

"I don't know."

"Where is he staying?"

"I don't know," Riley huffed. "I haven't asked yet, okay. What's with the interrogation?"

Scott's grip tightened around her arm.

Riley didn't like the way that he was looking at her.

It was the look that he had when he was talking to his charity cases.

"Don't you think that it's kinda suspicious," said Scott calmly. "That he just shows up out of the blue and suddenly has all this free time to spend with you and Ryan?"

"No, not if he's doing remote work or something."

"But why here?"

"Maybe he came for the scenery."

"In the off season?"

"What's your problem?" Riley ripped her arm out of his grip. "Are you jealous or something?"

"Jealous?" Scott laughed. "Why would I be jealous?"

"I dunno," Riley muttered. "Because there's suddenly someone who wants to spend time with me for a change. That things might actually start going well in my life. That I won't be one of your little damsels in distress anymore?"

"That's ridiculous," Scott scoffed. "I'm only looking out for you."

"Well maybe I don't need looking out for!"

"Look..I..." Scott was doing the nervous jaw rubbing thing again. "Have you ever heard of imprinting?"

"No."

"It happens with some animals, maybe werewolves too. They become insanely attached to someone and they can't let go."

Riley almost laughed. "You think that Elijah has imprinted on me."

"Perhaps."

"That's ridiculous," Riley scoffed. "He's not obsessed with me."

"And how would you know?"

"Well.......he's left me alone for years... and he hasn't once mentioned getting back together."

"Maybe it's all part of his plan? Maybe he's deliberately giving you space so that you'll let him in."

"That so stupid. Elijah's not like that."

"Really? And how would you know? From what you've told me about this guy, it sounds like you don't really know him either."

"You're unbelievable," Riley muttered and took a step back. "You just don't know when to stop."

Riley spun on her heels, walking back to the house.

"Ask him!" Scott yelled out after her. "Ask him what he's really doing out here."

"Fine!" Riley yelled back. "Maybe I will!"

"You'll see!"

"Just go home, Scott!"

Riley angrily wrapped her arms around her torso. She couldn't believe that Scott was being such an arse.

What did he know?

He'd barely even spoken to Elijah. He didn't know what sort of relationship Riley and Elijah had in the past. It wasn't as fucked up as what Abigail or Trissy went through.

Riley knew what was best for herself and Ryan. Scott needed to butt out and let her make her own decisions.

She could handle everything on her own.

CHAPTER SEVEN

The cafe was empty for most of the afternoon. There were only a few customers who stopped by for take-out coffee and one businessman who came to use the WiFi. He sat alone at a table typing, so most of Riley's shift was spent cleaning behind the counter.

Scott's annoying words echoed throughout Riley's head, making it difficult to concentrate.

She needed to have a talk with Scott about staying out of her business. He wasn't her father. He didn't have any right to tell her what to do.

Riley received a text message from Elijah towards the end of her shift.

Hey, Elijah wrote. *It was great spending time with you and Ryan today. I hope that I can see you both again soon.*

His words brought a small smile to Riley's face. She re-read the message several times.

Ask him what he's really doing out here, echoed Scott's words in her head.

Riley tried to push them back down into the depths of her mind, but they kept echoing back.

Ask him. Ask him. Ask him.

At least it would give her a reason to meet Elijah again.

Hey, Riley slowly typed back. *Are you free tonight or tomorrow? I'd like to meet you alone to talk more about Ryan.*

She sent the message, then slipped her phone back in her pocket.

It vibrated five minutes later.

I'm free tonight, Elijah wrote. *I'll come pick you up after your shift ends.*

Great, Riley wrote back. *I'll be outside waiting at five.*

Great. See you then, he wrote back.

Riley placed her phone down on the counter so that she wouldn't be tempted to keep looking at it.

Tonight she'd confront Elijah and prove to Scott that he was wrong.

There weren't many good places to eat in East Cove.

There was a Chinese restaurant owned by an elderly couple, and a takeaway store by the beach. It sold fish and chips along with various fried foods. It was cheap, so Riley usually brought some back for Ryan and the kids.

Riley bought a large fish and chips while Elijah waited in the car. She then directed him to a small park by the beach.

It was usually crowded during the summer, but it was mostly empty during the off season.

There was a small barbecue area full of wooden tables and chairs. It gave them a good view of the beach and the setting sun.

Two children were playing on a rusted swing set as their parents attempted to rustle them home for the day.

"Do you ever come here with Ryan?" Elijah asked as they sat down at a wooden table.

"Not yet." Riley slowly unwrapped the paper around the fish and chips. "It's hard to keep him from transforming, and he still doesn't like wearing clothes."

"So he just spends all his time at that farm?"

"Yeah, but we go to a lot of places nearby that don't have many people, like the mountains and some beaches."

"But nowhere far away?"

"We'll go once he's older." Riley shivered. She did up the buttons on her jacket to ward off the evening chill.

"It's difficult to raise a werewolf child so close to humans." Elijah munched on a fry. "There are too many differences. The elders don't allow it."

"Well, they're not here, are they," said Riley.

Mentions of werewolf society were enough to put her on edge. The more she learned about their ways, the more she came to dislike them.

Riley anxiously munched down several fries as she tried to think of what to say next.

It was time to cut the pointless small talk.

She needed to find out what Elijah was really doing in East Cove.

"So..." Riley tried to ask as casually as possible. "Where are you staying now?"

"There's a bunch of holiday villas on the way in. I've set up shop there for the time being."

"Yeah, I know the place," said Riley. "I did some cleaning there over the summer."

Elijah raised an eyebrow. "How many jobs do you have?"

"Just the coffee shop," said Riley. "But I do some other things during summer. More tourists come, so lots of work pops up."

"Sounds busy."

"Not really. It's all part-time and casual. It's hard to find any good full time work in this dump."

Elijah nodded like he was thinking her words over.

"What about you?" asked Riley. "What sort of work have you been doing out here?"

"Just making documents and answering calls," said Elijah. "The council wants to know about any werewolves living in the area."

"So you told them about us?"

"Not yet." He picked up a piece of fish and took a bite. "Would you prefer if I don't?"

"Of course." She almost laughed. "I don't want those people knowing anything about me."

"But they can help you," said Elijah. "Werewolves should stick together."

"Why?" said Riley. "So that they can control my life and take my kid?"

"It's not like that," said Elijah. "They'd never remove a child from their family without a good reason."

"Are you sure?"

"I won't let it happen," said Elijah. "I promise."

He seemed sincere, but Riley found it difficult to believe.

"I don't want those people to know anything about Ryan," she said.

"Why? They're his family too."

"But I'm the one who raised him," said Riley. "He's my son."

"But he'd be better off amongst real werewolves. You're just suppressing his potential by forcing him to be human."

"I'm not forcing him to be human."

"Yes, you are. You shouldn't be hiding him away out here with those people."

"Those people are my friends."

"But not one of them is a real werewolf. They don't know how to raise him properly. If you come back with me I can help you both."

"I don't need your help." Riley crossed her arms over her chest as anger began to build. "We're doing fine here."

"Really, because you don't look it. You're living in this shitty town in the middle of nowhere, sharing a crowded shack, and cleaning like a maid."

Riley was too shocked to speak.

What the fuck did he just say?

Elijah hadn't changed.

He hadn't changed at all.

He was still the same pretentious stuck up arsehole that she knew five years ago.

"These people have clearly brainwashed you," Elijah continued, oblivious to her horror. "You're a werewolf now. You shouldn't be forced to live this way."

"*How dare you*," Riley hissed. "How dare you come back into my life and tell me what to do." She quickly gathered her things and stood to her feet. "This was all a mistake."

She moved to leave, but Elijah's hand quickly lunged out to grab her wrist.

"No, please," he begged. "Please don't leave."

Riley tugged her arm. "Let go of me, Elijah."

"No, please." Elijah said. "Don't go."

"I'll scream for help."

"I can't live without you!"

It sounded so outrageous that Riley stopped fighting him. "What?"

Elijah anxiously looked away like he was too embarrassed to make eye contact, mouth opening and closing as he searched for words.

"I couldn't be the same....after you left," he said softly. "It always felt like part of me was missing.... until I saw you again."

"That's ridiculous." Riley ripped her arm out of his grip. "We were barely together and I haven't seen you in years."

"It doesn't matter," said Elijah. "I thought that I could forget you, but no matter how hard I try it doesn't get better. I *need* you."

"You need a therapist!" Riley snapped.

"It didn't work." Elijah angrily tugged on his hair. "Nothing works, because we're fated ma-"

"Not this shit again," Riley moaned.

"I know that you feel it too," Elijah begged.

"No, I don't!" Riley snapped, but it wasn't a complete lie.

She did feel an urge. A strange pulling towards him. He consumed her thoughts and her dreams, but it didn't control her. Riley's human mind could reason that such feelings were stupid and that she shouldn't give into them.

Unlike Elijah, she was fully in control of her own shit.

"I don't feel anything," Riley lied.

"That's because they've drugged you," Elijah said. "I can smell it. If you only embraced your true self then you'd understand that-"

"Enough!" Riley said. "I don't want to hear it."

"Riley-"

"Just go home, Elijah." Riley took a step back, putting some distance between them. "Nothing's going to happen between us."

"What about Ryan?"

"I'll call you, and maybe we can work something out, but first I need some space."

"No." He shook his head. "It's never going to work. We have to be together."

"Grow up!" Riley yelled back. "I don't belong to you. You can't just waltz into my life and expect me to throw myself at your feet. Just leave me alone like a decent human being!"

Elijah was lost for words.

He looked taken back for a moment, but then angrily crossed his arms like a spoiled child who'd just been punished.

"Fine," Elijah angrily muttered.

Finally, Riley thought. At least he wasn't impossible.

"If you won't listen," said Elijah. "Then I'll just have to make you understand."

A cold chill ran down Riley's spine.

She needed to leave.

"Goodbye, Elijah." Riley took one step in front of the other. "I'll call you when I'm ready."

Elijah didn't say anything.

Riley quickly glanced over her shoulder to see that he hadn't moved, silently watching her with an unreadable expression.

What had she done?

CHAPTER EIGHT

"He did what?" echoed Scott's voice over the phone.

Riley took a seat on her bed. She was already dressed for bed in pink flannel pajamas.

"I said that he tried to get back together," said Riley.

She peered through the open door to see Ryan playing with Trissy's children in the living room.

"*Motherfucker*," Scott hissed over the phone.

"Right," Riley said. "He was spewing all that *fated mates* bullshit that he loves so much."

"I told you that it was imprinting."

"Yeah..maybe.." Riley sighed. "I feel like such an idiot."

"Don't blame yourself. You're not the first woman who's been tricked by a crazy ex."

"He's not crazy.....he's just...."

Riley searched for the right word to describe Elijah. He reminded her of a spoiled puppy refusing to let go of a toy.

"Persistent," Riley said. "He has all these ideas in his head, and he doesn't understand why I don't think the same."

"Sounds like he's in pretty deep."

"He's surrounded by assholes who think they're part of some master race." Riley pulled back the curtain to peer out the window. "It's impossible to get through to him."

"Maybe I should come over," said Scott.

"No, it's okay. Elijah's an entitled prick, but I can't imagine him doing anything extreme."

"Are you sure?"

"Yeah. I'm just worried about him showing up here or work."

There was something about Elijah's face that hinted that he wouldn't take no for an answer.

"I'll drop by tomorrow," said Scott. "Jacob won't stop talking about his lego ship anyway."

"Are you sure? What about Abigail?"

"She'll be fine. Her hormones are starting to balance out more. She was talking today about heading back home in another week or so."

"That's good."

"So I'll have plenty of time to be your knight in shining armor."

"You wish," Riley scoffed.

"I'll see you in the morning."

"Okay. Thanks for everything Scott."

"Don't worry about it. Just take care of yourself."

"Will do."

"Night, Riley."

"Night, Scott."

Riley hung up the call and collapsed back onto the bed.

She scrolled through her phone, checking the news and weather for the fourth time that evening. She was tempted to look Elijah up on social media, but then decided against it.

Seeing his face would only make her think ridiculous things.

Why did she bring this clusterfuck down on herself?

The pounding of small footsteps echoed up the hallway towards her.

Riley looked up to see Ryan enthusiastically waving a crayon drawing in her face.

"Hey," Riley said with a smile. "What do you have there?"

Ryan passed her the drawing. It was a large pink circle with yellow hair, standing next to a large blob that she assumed was a car.

"Oh," said Riley anxiously, hoping that it wasn't what it looked like. "Is that Daddy?"

Ryan enthusiastically nodded.

"Oh...wow." Riley internally swore. "It's great."

Ryan made a long string of hand gestures that Riley found hard to understand. He jabbed one finger towards her phone, then pointed to his picture.

"Well, Daddy is a very busy man," said Riley, but the look of disappointment on Ryan's face was almost enough to break her. "But I'm sure that we'll see him again sometime."

Hopefully when he stops being a fucking weirdo, Riley didn't dare say out loud.

"How about you go brush your teeth," said Riley. "It's bedtime soon."

Ryan shook his head and dashed back down the hall. He crawled under the sofa in a poor attempt to hide.

Riley sighed and got to her feet.

After an hour of struggling to make Ryan brush his teeth and put on his pajamas, Riley finally managed to wrangle Ryan into his own bed.

Riley lay down beside him as she read a bright picture book.

"Goodnight bunny," Riley said while pointing to the cartoonish pictures. "Goodnight toothbrush. Goodnight grass."

Ryan ripped the book out of her hand and began to flip through the pages on his own.

Riley yawned and turned off the light. She pretended to be asleep until Ryan dozed off beside her.

There were still things that she needed to do, but Riley was too tired to move. She pulled a blanket over her shoulders and drifted off to sleep.

Riley felt her body rock back and forth as she was carried through darkness. She could hear the rustling of wind through the trees, and dried grass crunching under large shoes.

The cold night air chilled her skin.

Riley shivered.

Strong arms pulled her closer. A warm chest pressed against her cheek.

She knew that smell.

"Elijah?" Riley whispered.

"It's okay." His deep voice rumbled down to her core. "Just go back to sleep."

Her body felt light and fuzzy.

Was this real or just another dream?

"What are you doing?" she mumbled.

Riley cracked open her eyes to see the starry sky above them as Elijah carried her through an overgrown field.

"I'll show you," he said with conviction. "I'll show you everything."

The gentle swaying of her body in Elijah's arms slowly lured Riley back into unconsciousness.

It was okay.

Elijah couldn't really be there.

When she woke up everything would be back to normal.

CHAPTER NINE

Riley was awoken by sunlight filtering into the room.

She shifted under the blankets, snuggling up to a pillow in search of more sleep. She needed to get as much rest as possible before Ryan woke up.

But something was off.

It was quiet.

Far too quiet.

Riley was usually awoken by the screaming of children, or Ryan climbing all over her. She could usually hear people walking around the house or the T.V blaring cartoons in the living room.

But there was nothing.

Not even the gentle breathing of her son sleeping in his bed.

Riley shot up, quickly scanning her surroundings.

It was not her fucking room.

The floor was covered in spotless white carpet, and the furniture was all made from wood. The floral curtains and wallpaper were well coordinated and there wasn't a single toy in sight.

Riley was sitting on a large double bed with pristine pink sheets. There was a white tiled bathroom between two double doors.

What the fuck was happening?

Riley didn't have long to think before another door swung open.

Her whole body tensed. She backed up against the pillows as her fight or flight response kicked in.

In walked Elijah carrying a large tray of food. He placed it down on the bed before her.

There were scrambled eggs and sausages, along with a small stack of pancakes.

The whole scene threw Riley off balance.

"I thought you might be hungry," Elijah said cheerfully, like nothing was wrong. "So I brought you some food."

Riley's stomach let out a small growl, but she was too mortified to touch it.

"What is this place?" she asked, voice trembling

"My home.. well our home," he said.

Riley could feel panic bubbling back to the surface.

"How did I even get here?" She looked down at her pajamas, relieved to find that nothing was out of place. "Did you.....Did you kidnap me?"

"I didn't have a choice," said Elijah. "It was the only way to make you leave."

"I didn't need to leave!" she angrily snapped.

"Those people weren't good for you," said Elijah. "They were filling your head with lies, drugging you, and turning you against me."

"Do you seriously believe all the shit that comes out of your mouth?"

"You're safe now," Elijah said like she was the one who was nuts. "I'll help you. We can fix this together."

He reached for her hand but Riley pulled it back.

"I don't need your help," she said.

"Riley-"

"Just stay away." Riley scrambled backwards until she reached the other side of the bed.

"Riley-"

Riley dashed for the door, slipping outside before he could follow.

She ran down a long hallway until she reached a set of wide stairs, jumping down two at a time towards a marble entrance hall.

She threw open the front door and ran past an expensive car and well maintained gardens, dashing down a long stone driveway and through two large iron gates.

Riley had no idea where she was.

She decided to follow the road until she reached a town, then work it out from there.

She walked barefoot down the mountain, ducking into the bushes to hide when she heard a car coming.

She passed several driveways leading up to unmarked buildings or mansions, but she didn't feel like she could trust the people inside.

What if they were werewolves too? What if they took her straight back to Elijah?

She needed to get back to East Cove and Ryan.

After hours of walking, she spotted a small town.

There was a cluster of houses and an old fashioned main street. The tin roofs were rusted and there were several crumbling homes, but it didn't look any different to other country towns that Riley had passed on her travels.

She slowly walked towards the gas station, deciding that it was the safest place to ask for directions and find a way back to East Cove.

It was impossible to avoid the curious stares of several people who walked past. They quietly muttered to each other while glancing back at her.

Riley assumed it was because she was still dressed in her pajamas.

But the sight of a wolf casually walking down the road made her insides freeze.

No. It couldn't be.

Several townspeople emerged from their homes to stare, like they'd never seen an outsider before.

They looked like regular people, but Riley could tell that something was off.

They didn't smell human.

"What's she doing here?" Riley heard someone mutter.

"An outsider?"

"No, she has the wolf. I can smell it on her."

"Is she from up the hill?"

"She doesn't look like them."

"What should we do about her?"

Riley backed away, fear flooding her mind.

No.

They were all werewolves.

She spun on her heels and dashed down the road, trying to get away as fast as possible.

The forest! Her instincts screamed.

Riley dashed to the side of the road, running through an overgrown car park and then into the bushes. Stray branches scratched her face.

She glanced over her shoulder, but no one was following.

She felt too afraid to let her guard down, plunging deeper into the woods.

Riley soon discovered that she was shit at navigating her way through the undergrowth. She pushed her way through the bushes and climbed over large rocks and vines, searching for anything that could give her a hint to where she was going.

Riley hadn't been paying proper attention when she blindly dashed into its depths, throwing her sense of direction off.

Things would have been easier if she had her phone, but it was probably back in her room in East Cove, along with Ryan and all of her things.

Riley hoped that her son was okay. He had Trissy, Vanessa and Scott, so hopefully he'd be fine.

What the fuck was Elijah thinking? How could he possibly assume that kidnapping her would be a good idea? Did he expect her to just bow down before him and merrily suck his dick?

"Fucking werewolves," Riley swore under her breath while pushing a large branch out of the way.

As soon as she got back to East Cove, she would grab Ryan and take him away. Somewhere far where Elijah would never find them.

She'd be perfectly content never seeing that fucker again.

Riley sat down on a fallen tree trunk to take a break. Her feet were scratched and aching from walking without shoes.

The forest was silent except for the chirping of birds and the rustling of wind moving through the trees. Nobody was coming after her.

It was pointless to keep moving forward without any direction. There was no telling how much further the forest extended. She could spend days walking and not reach anything.

She needed to go back to the main road.

Riley laid back against the tree trunk and sighed, closing her eyes to try and get some rest. There was no telling when she'd next get the chance.

The longer she sat there, the louder the forest became around her.

Riley could hear the humming of insects and the footsteps of distant animals. She could smell which creatures had passed through the area. If she just followed their scent, she could find her next meal.

She longed to sink her teeth into something delicious and warm. The smell of rabbit and possum was enough to make her mouth water.

That's when it hit Riley.

It had been more than a day since she'd last consumed her medication.

Her werewolf senses were slowly coming back.

"Fuck," Riley swore and got to her feet.

There wasn't any time.

The longer she waited, the more that she risked having her mind taken over by *it*.

The wolf inside her.

Riley could feel it clawing to the surface. Furious after being contained for so long. It wanted to run, hunt, and howl under the moon, taking everything that it had craved for so long.

It wanted *him*.

Riley quickly walked, trying to retrace her steps, but she collapsed to her knees when a strange spasm hit her body.

She threw her arms out to support her own weight, only to look down and see that her right arm was covered in grey fur.

"No," Riley muttered, begging it to stop. "No, please, not now."

Riley refused to let the animal take control.

She gasped as her body began to change, bones breaking and reshaping like they had a life of their own.

Fur sprouted from her skin as her body shrunk, large teeth extending from her jaw as claws emerged from her hand.

In a matter of seconds, Riley was gone.

In her place stood a large grey wolf.

CHAPTER TEN

Time didn't have any meaning.

Sometimes Riley felt flashes of her human consciousness, but they were few and far between.

The wolf had taken control.

After being cooped up for years, it selfishly refused to relinquish the body.

It hunted amongst the thick forest, ripping apart small animals and devouring their insides. It played in the river and dozed outside under the moon.

It was one with the natural world.

All human things were unnecessary and pointless.

In a rare flash of consciousness, Riley took the opportunity to return to her human form.

She shifted back into her human skin only to find that she was completely naked.

Her skin was covered in dirt and there was dried blood under her nails. The scratches on her feet were gone, indicating that some time had passed.

Riley shivered in the evening chill, wrapping her thin arms around her torso.

She needed to find somewhere.

Anywhere.

She slowly put one foot in front of the other, struggling to gain her balance like her body wasn't used to walking on two legs.

She spotted a fresh animal carcass a few feet away. Her stomach felt full like it was her last meal.

Disgusting, Riley would have said a week earlier, but now the smell was enticing. Part of her wanted to rip straight into it and pick the meat from the bones.

"No," Riley muttered to herself. "This isn't me."

She just needed to find a way back to civilization and get help. Once she was amongst regular people, she could find her way back to East Cove and get more medication.

Just try and breathe, Riley remembered Wanda's words from years earlier. *The wolf will only lash out if you try to fight it. You need to follow your instincts and try to keep it happy.*

"Fuck that shit," Riley muttered, but she tried to relax and absorb the sounds and smells around her. It helped her to regain control when she first became a werewolf.

Animal-like thoughts filtered into her brain.

Hunt.

Eat.

Breed.

Him.

The last one caused Riley to shiver as a jab of arousal went through her groin.

No. That was the last thing she wanted.

She didn't need Elijah.

Riley soon found a river.

She used the cold water to wash the dirt and grime from her body, trying to regain some semblance of her human self.

But it didn't stop the uncomfortable pulsing between her legs.

It was like a hunger, clawing at her from the inside, urging her to seek out *him* and join her body with *his.*

The wolf didn't seem to care how badly he'd screwed her over. It was fine with being that psycho's cum bucket.

Fucking werewolf hormones, Riley swore to herself.

She tried to ignore it, but the space between her legs was dripping, smearing her thighs with her own warm fluids. It became uncomfortable every time that she moved.

She tried to submerge her body in the river to cool the heat building inside her, but the water was freezing. She could only manage a few minutes before quickly hopping out.

The sun was low in the sky.

Riley doubted that she'd reach anywhere by nightfall. She decided to concentrate on making shelter for the night.

She knew that keeping warm would be easier in wolf form, but she didn't trust her inner animal.

What if it refused to relinquish control again?

Riley gathered materials to make a fire. It took several attempts to get the flames going, but she managed to light it using techniques that Wanda once taught her.

She created a small bed of leaves and curled up close to the fire, letting the warmth wash over her chilled skin.

It was only then that she realized how exhausted her body felt. Riley passed out as the sounds of the forest gradually lured her to sleep.

Riley awoke in the middle of the night.

The forest was still dark, and the fire had burnt down to embers. Hours must have passed since she fell asleep.

Riley shifted uncomfortably. The leaves rustled around her body.

It felt like she was burning up.

It was like someone had ignited a fire in her core.

Her breasts felt rock hard and the space between her legs was soaked.

Her groin pulsed, begging for friction.

She tossed and turned, trying to ignore it and get back to sleep, but the need between her legs was all she could think of.

Riley rolled onto her back and spread her legs wide, slipping one hand between her thighs to where it was most needed.

She hissed in relief, mouth curving up into a smile.

She ran her fingers through the wet heat, spreading warm fluid over her engorged clit, jolting at the sudden onset of sensation.

Fuck, that felt good.

Once Riley started, it was impossible to stop.

She arched her back as pleasure grew in her core, erasing all reasonable thoughts from her mind.

More...

She rolled onto her hands and knees, smooth arse thrust in the air.

She plunged a wet hand back between her legs, not bothering to suppress her moans as she worked herself up.

Just a little more...

A warm hand pressed against her plush arse.

Riley didn't need to look to know who it was.

"Do you remember now?" said Elijah as he draped himself over her naked body.

He slipped his rock hard cock into her dripping pussy, pressing all the way in until he was flush against her.

"*Ah,*" Elijah sighed. "That feels so much better."

Riley wasn't sure how to react.

It felt natural to have his large naked body pressed against her, to have his cock deep inside until it touched her cervix.

It felt like the past five years never happened.

"*I missed this,*" Elijah whispered as he began to thrust. "No one ever felt as good as you."

Riley remained silent, too overwhelmed by the sensations pulsing through her limbs.

Why did it feel so good?

"We'll be together," huffed Elijah. "You, me, and Ryan. He's waiting for you back at the house. I'd never take him away from you. Remember how I promised you that?"

Ryan...

Riley felt relieved that he was nearby.

Riley gasped as she was hit by a strong wave of sensation. "What about your family?"

"Don't worry about them," Elijah said with a roll of his hips. He pressed his lips to her neck, then moved one hand between her legs to rub her clit. "Let's just live in this moment."

Riley knew that he was lying. She doubted that anything had changed. This was a werewolf community, so his relatives couldn't be far away.

Riley thought of pushing Elijah away, but her human logic was dulled by all the werewolf urges.

It was overjoyed to have his thick cock deep inside her.

It wanted to screw him again and again until they were both spent.

Riley's human self was slowly being pushed deeper and deeper into the back of her own mind.

With a growl, Riley pushed Elijah back and flipped their positions, grabbing his wrists and pinning him to the ground.

Elijah's eyes went wide with surprise.

She sank down onto his rock hard erection, bringing it deep inside until her pelvis was flush against his.

Yes. This was what she needed.

This was how they were supposed to be.

Riley rocked against him, chasing addictive pleasure as Elijah trembled beneath her.

He hissed as his face screwed up with pleasure. "Yes...just like that."

Every slide of her clit against him felt like heaven.

Watching her body bring him pleasure made Riley feel powerful.

She didn't relent as her groin went numb, signaling her oncoming orgasm. She sped up the pace until her climax exploded outwards, washing over her body.

Her insides pulsed and tightened around him, pulling Elijah over the edge.

He groaned as he climaxed, spilling his warm seed into her body, just like the wolf wanted.

The wolf didn't care about stupid human traditions. It would take what it wanted from Elijah and more, using his body to help create her new young.

They'd stay together and breed for as long as possible, spawning new children in the spring.

The wolf had no intention of leaving him and returning to human society.

It understood that they were fated mates.

WEREWOLF BREEDING ACADEMY 3

BY BEATRIX ARDEN

CHAPTER ONE

Riley surveyed the mountainside from her window, taking in the dark forest and full moon. Rolling hills extended as far as she could see. The distant howls of wolves echoed throughout the trees.

Riley toyed with the gold chain around her neck.

Elijah placed it there while she was sleeping. He showered her in gifts in a poor attempt to make up for the kidnapping.

The double bed behind Riley was lined with red silk sheets, and there was a closet stuffed with expensive dresses. Several gold chains and bracelets were littered throughout the room.

But all of it meant nothing to Riley.

She'd give it all up for the chance to return to her old life.

Riley groaned and wiped the sweat from her forehead.

Her body was bare except for a short lace nightgown, leaving her tanned arms and legs fully exposed, but she didn't feel the evening chill.

Quite the opposite.

It felt like her body was on fire.

A fever burned deep inside her, causing abnormal heat to radiate from her skin. Her dark hair was plastered to her nape with sweat.

Riley looked to the forest as she tried to distract herself from the hunger that was steadily growing between her legs.

Her sex pulsed with need. All she could think of was slipping her fingers deep inside to relieve the discomfort.

Did Rapunzel ever wank while she was trapped in the tower? Riley thought.

Holding back was excruciating.

Riley slipped one hand between her thighs, sighing in relief the moment that it touched her swollen clit. She slowly rubbed her fingers back and forth, creating delicious pressure with every slide.

So good....

Riley groaned as pleasure bloomed from her center. She slumped back in the chair and spread her legs wider, creating more friction against her clit.

Her pussy was already dripping, providing the perfect warm lubricant to get off.

Riley hissed as her hand shamelessly rubbed back and forth along her groin, trying to stimulate as many areas at once.

More...

Riley's other hand reached down to palm a breast, gently squeezing as she rode wave after wave of joyous sensation.

Why did she ever try to fight something so wonderful?

Riley didn't care if there was anyone outside listening. All that mattered was reaching the end.

She sent herself speeding towards climax, gasping as mind numbing pleasure exploded from her core.

Riley curled in on herself, gasping for breath as her body shook.

That's better...

A warm haze washed over her mind. Riley lay back in the chair, lazily staring up at the moon as she basked in the aftermath of her orgasm.

The need had abated, but it was still there, whispering in the back of her mind like the wolf that had invaded her body.

"Beautiful, isn't it?" said a deep voice from the doorway. "Isn't it easier when you don't have to hide from yourself?"

Riley didn't need to turn to see who it was.

Elijah walked across the room. He wrapped his strong arms around Riley from behind, burying his warm face against her exposed neck.

He was shirtless, body heat melting into hers. The moonlight illuminated his pale skin and broad chest. His short blond hair was damp like he'd just gotten out of the shower.

*Him...*hummed the stupid wolf who lived in Riley's head, overjoyed that her mate had come to play.

Riley fought the urge to smile, but she couldn't hide her body's reaction.

Her back instinctively arched into his touch.

Riley's swollen sex pulsed with anticipation, dripping in preparation to accept his engorged shaft.

That was all the encouragement that Elijah needed. His warm lips pressed against Riley's throat, sending delicious tingles of pleasure straight down to her groin.

Riley gasped and closed her eyes, giving into the sensations pulsing through her skin.

There was no point trying to fight it.

Elijah's large hand reached around her torso to cup a breast. He gently massaged the skin through her dress before slipping his fingers under her bra, running along her nipple.

Riley tilted her head back, allowing Elijah's lips to crush against hers.

His large fingers slid into her hair, tilting her head as his tongue pressed past her lips.

There was no hesitation. He confidently took what he wanted like it was the most natural thing in the world, exploring her mouth as Riley moaned.

More, she wanted to beg, rubbing her thighs together in a poor attempt to ease the hunger.

Elijah pulled away. He hooked his arms under Riley's legs and carried her over to the bed, laying her down on the ruffled sheets.

Riley watched Elijah slip off his jeans, hungrily admiring his bare skin.

She would never tire of seeing him naked. Elijah's shaft was already fully erect, twitching with need between his large thighs.

Mine.... Riley's mind sang while gazing in awe at his rippling muscles and swollen dick.

She settled back against the sheets, spreading her legs wide to invite him inside her.

Elijah climbed over her thin body, settling between her thighs as he pulled the nightdress up over her breasts. He ran his warm tongue over her nipples, licking and sucking as Riley slid her hands through his damp hair.

His naked chest pressed against her as he returned his lips to her throat, covering it in kisses as his erection rubbed the outside of her sex.

Riley gasped and arched her head back, spreading her legs further to get more friction against her aching clit.

All doubts disappeared when he was pressed against her, working her feverish body up to an intoxicating high.

The tip of his cock caught on her damp entrance, then slowly pushed in, bottoming out with little resistance.

Elijah paused to savor the sensation, letting out a sigh as her entrance tightly hugged his swollen shaft.

Riley moaned and rolled her hips, urging him to move.

Elijah slowly pulled out, then thrust back inside, hitting deep within her core. He tightly clasped her hand, watching her face contort in pleasure.

Riley let out small gasps, squeezing his fingers every time that she was hit with a strong jolt of sensation.

Why did it always feel so good?

Elijah was clearly a fascist monster, but none of that mattered when he was buried deep within her.

Riley sighed and gripped his hand tighter, losing herself in the moment.

CHAPTER TWO

It was when she was alone, that Riley's common sense kicked in.

Living with Elijah in an isolated mountain community wasn't what she wanted. She was surrounded by werewolves who were all on his side.

Being a single mother back in East Cove was hard, but at least she had friends and full control of her mind.

Without medication, it felt like a wild animal had been shoved into her skull. She never knew when the werewolf inside her would suddenly take the wheel.

Riley slipped out of bed as Elijah slept.

He shifted and groaned like he could sense her absence, smooth naked torso moving with each gentle breath.

Just the thought of leaving Elijah was painful, but Riley needed to get away before it was too late. She could already feel herself become more attached with each coming day.

It was like their souls were slowly meshing together.

If Riley stayed any longer, she would fool herself into thinking that she had feelings for her kidnapper.

It was dangerous to trust him.

Riley quickly gathered her clothes from the floor and slipped them on. She silently moved through the mansion and out the front door.

The full moon illuminated a desolate road of dark houses. The concrete was damp under Riley's toes as the need to hunt pulsed through her veins.

She fought the urge to transform, shoving the wolf to the back of her mind.

This isn't the time to go frolic in the fucking forest like a dog, she thought to herself.

The wolf in her brain didn't like being ignored.

It would take what it wanted whether Riley liked it or not.

"*No, no, no,*" Riley hissed and fell to her knees, failing to stop the oncoming change.

Her bones cracked and moved as grey fur covered her skin. Sharp teeth descended from her jaw and claws sprung from her fingers.

In less than a minute, Riley was gone. In her place stood a large grey wolf.

Riley awoke hours later in the forest. The surrounding trees were unfamiliar and the cries of night animals echoed around her.

Fresh blood dripped from Riley's mouth, down her naked chest and stomach. She could taste raw rabbit on her tongue.

Delicious...

A naked Elijah stood before her, eyes wide in awe as he admired her disheveled hair and blood stained body.

Him.. hummed the stupid wolf within her.

Her apex pulsed with need.

Riley approached him like another prey, hungry sex throbbing between her drenched thighs.

She wrapped her arms around Elijah's neck and crushed her mouth to his, smearing blood across his lips.

Elijah didn't protest, eagerly accepting her. His growing erection pressed against her lower body.

He didn't fight back when Riley shoved him to the forest floor.

She sank down onto his swollen shaft, using his hard cock to satisfy her hunger.

Elijah moaned and gripped her thighs, allowing Riley to take what she wanted.

Pressure grew in her apex with each rough slide. Nothing mattered except reaching the end.

The wolf inside Riley sang. It was overjoyed to be breeding with its mate.

It didn't care about birth control or protection. All it wanted was to use Elijah's strong body to reproduce.

Riley felt like a passenger in her own skin.

"*I'm close,*" Elijah hissed as he tried to hold back his orgasm, gripping her tighter.

Riley nodded and sped up, chasing her own climax.

Elijah came with a groan, pumping his strong hips up into her body as cum sprayed from his dick.

Riley wasn't far behind. She rocked against his body until her groin went numb, sending her spiraling towards an all consuming orgasm.

Then she crashed, rapidly rocking herself on Elijah's cock as her pulsing passage sucked his cum deeper.

Riley had done plenty of crazy wolf fucking with Elijah in the past, but this time felt different.

There was a hunger inside her she'd never felt before. An insatiable need that wasn't easily quenched.

It didn't matter if they spent a whole evening screwing on the forest floor like animals. All she wanted was to feel him deep inside her.

She'd never experienced such an insane lack of control.

"What is this?" Riley asked.

Elijah had her pinned against the shower wall, slowly thrusting into her from behind.

"It's your heat," he said, licking droplets of water from her neck.

"Heat?"

"It happens to female wolves a few times a year." He pushed his cock in deep, then paused to savor the feeling. "They get the overwhelming need to breed."

"But this..... has never happened before," Riley gasped.

"That's because you were taking those shitty drugs. It threw your body off....now it's working hard to catch up."

There was still so much that Riley wanted to ask, but Elijah slipped a hand between her legs to stimulate her clit, causing her to jolt with pleasure.

"Don't worry, Riley." Elijah pressed his warm lips to her neck. "I'll take care of you like a good mate."

Riley nodded, crying out as she came hard around his cock.

"*Shit*," Elijah hissed and rapidly pumped his hips until he came, spilling his essence deep inside her.

CHAPTER THREE

Riley could tell when her heat was over. The fever was gone and the pulsing between her thighs gradually subsided.

She felt somewhat human again for the first time in days.

She rolled over in bed to find Elijah gone and the house silent. He often disappeared without telling her why, but she pretended that it didn't bother her.

Riley glanced longingly at the window. She wanted to attempt another escape, but it was pointless to anger her inner wolf again.

The needy bitch seemed overjoyed that Elijah was nearby and didn't want to go. If Riley tried to leave, it would only force another transformation and run wild again, prancing all over the forest, then coming back to fuck Elijah's brains out.

It wasn't rare for human born werewolves to completely lose to the animal. Riley had spent months roaming the mountains as a wolf after her first transformation.

The only way to peacefully co-exist with the wolf was for Riley to follow the shitty animal urges. She had to go along with what it wanted until she thought of another way to escape.

Even if it meant staying in Elijah's home.

Riley took a bath and dressed for the day. She pulled her hair back into a bun and slipped on a thin summer dress that had been laid out on the bed.

Riley took a step outside the bedroom, trying to put on a brave face.

Just pretend that you give a shit about being here, she told herself. *Things will only be harder if they know you want to escape.*

Riley wandered around the house, looking for any signs of life. There were two empty bedrooms, a large living room, and a kitchen. The whole place was decked out in expensive carpets and furniture that barely looked used.

The kitchen was full of shiny appliances that she'd only dreamed of owning.

Riley opened the fridge door to find a whole cooked chicken.

Her stomach growled.

Riley dug into it with vigor, ripping parts of the chicken off with her fingers, hungrily shoving them into her mouth. She was famished after only eating wild animals during her heat.

Tall heels clicked against the kitchen tiles behind her.

"Well, if it's not Elijah's little cum dumpster," said a familiar high pitched voice.

Riley jumped. She turned to see Latavia standing behind the counter.

Latavia's make-up was flawless and her pale hair was pulled back into an immaculate braid. The low collar of her floral dress flaunted her generous cleavage.

"Latavia," Riley sighed, not surprised to see Elijah's old girlfriend hanging around.

"Still as feral as always." Latavia ran her gaze over Riley's wet hair and unshaven legs. "My parents wouldn't have spent so much on my upbringing if they'd known that shamelessly stuffing my face was enough to make Elijah hard."

"What are you doing here?" Riley sighed. She didn't have the patience to put up with Latavia's shit.

"Just visiting my husband, of course."

Riley's stomach dropped.

No. It couldn't be possible.

Latavia's laugh echoed throughout the kitchen. "Oh, so he didn't tell you?"

"Tell me what?"

"Elijah and I are married of course." Latavia extended one pale hand to show off a glimmering diamond ring. "It was a wonderful wedding. Too bad you couldn't make it."

Riley stared at the large gem. Rage ignited in her stomach.

Motherfucker, Riley swore to herself.

She should have known that Elijah was full of shit. Of course he had married Latavia.

Latavia's mouth curved into a brilliant smile, basking in Riley's anguish.

"And there's even more wonderful news," she said playfully. She pulled her dress taunt over her stomach, showing off an obvious baby bump. "I'm already six months along. Elijah is so looking forward to meeting the baby. We both agree that they'll be a wonderful little sibling for all our other children."

Riley was too stunned for words, gazing at Latavia's stomach in horror.

Elijah was a dead man.

Riley was going to rip him to pieces and scatter his entrails over the mountainside.

Latavia didn't hide her smugness. The bitch looked like Christmas had come early.

"Tata for now, muncher trash," she said and spun on her heels. "The baby shower is waiting."

Latavia's laughter echoed throughout the hallway until she closed the front door behind her.

Riley was too livid to eat. She angrily paced the living room, waiting for Elijah to return.

She shouldn't have been surprised.

Riley assumed that Elijah and Latavia fucked like rabbits while she was gone, pumping out several new offspring. Maybe that was why Elijah dumped Riley in a separate house that barely looked used. He planned on keeping her locked away as a side piece while he returned to his main family every morning.

Riley was a fool for believing that he had been truthful about something.

Elijah returned an hour later. Riley stormed towards him the moment that he walked through the door.

His mouth curved into a smile, but it quickly disappeared when he saw her furious expression.

"You married Latavia?" Riley angrily snapped.

Elijah's gaze fell to the floor. He sighed and ran a hand through his hair. "It was already arranged......and you were gone.....so I had to go through with the wedding."

"Then why the hell did you tell me that you were separated?"

"We are. We started living apart soon afterwards."

"Except when you're getting her pregnant?"

"What do you mean?"

"She was here, Elijah....looking all knocked up and shit."

"That's not my kid," he laughed. "We haven't had sex in years."

"Then whose baby is it?"

Elijah shrugged. "Who knows..... She's always been popular with the family."

Those words sent an uneasy shiver through Riley's body.

She was assaulted by the mental image of Latavia being passed around various men, but Riley quickly pushed any sympathy to the back of her mind.

Latavia was a selfish bitch who would happily screw anyone.

Elijah looked into Riley's eyes. "We're not together anymore," he said softly. "I promise."

Riley bit her lower lip as she tried to work out if Elijah was being truthful. She wanted to believe him, but it sounded like another ploy to stop her from leaving.

Elijah was like a needy child who didn't want his favorite toy taken away. She had no idea what kind of crazy shit he would do to stop her from leaving.

"Come on." Elijah reached out and took hold of Riley's hand. "There's something that I want to show you."

Riley tugged her hand out of his grasp. "What is it?"

"Ryan."

"Ryan?"

It had been over a week since Riley last saw her son. Elijah had given vague answers every time she asked about him.

"Is he alright?" Riley asked. "Where is he?"

"We can go see him now," said Elijah.

Riley was still pissed, but the prospect of seeing her son was too enticing to pass up.

She let Elijah take hold of her hand and lead her out of the house.

He gently squeezed her fingers. "We could get there faster if we transform."

"No," said Riley.

Her inner wolf was stronger when she transformed. She couldn't trust it not to jump Elijah's bones when she was supposed to be giving him the cold shoulder.

"Okay," Elijah sighed. "We can walk."

The main road was full of spacious mansions, but a short walk through the woods led to dirt roads full of older houses.

Many of the young people resembled Elijah with blond hair and blue eyes. They wore loose fitting clothes or moved around in wolf form.

"Is this where you grew up?" Riley asked.

"Yes," said Elijah. "Isn't it beautiful?"

"Like an Nazi wet dream?"

"What does that mean?"

"Don't worry," said Riley. She didn't expect him to understand. "Did you seriously spend your whole life here?"

"Some of it. I traveled with my grandfather between other clans. He wanted me to learn about our society as much as possible."

Riley wanted to ask more, until she was distracted by a young couple screwing against a tree.

The woman was stark naked as a hairy guy pounded into her from behind. There was another man standing beside them, massaging his cock like he was waiting his turn.

Riley quickly averted her gaze.

She'd forgotten about the creepy public screwing. Back at the academy, the students were encouraged to reproduce as much as possible, fucking all over the classroom and grounds.

Elijah's blond cult village was obviously no different.

Elijah wrapped an arm around Riley's shoulders to pull her closer. "I don't know why you're always so embarrassed." His warm lips brushed her ear. "It's only natural."

Riley shivered and crossed her arms. "There's nothing wrong with getting a room."

"But it's hot to screw you where everyone can see."

Riley shoved him away. They were not going to have sex in the middle of the village.

Elijah let out a sigh of disappointment and rubbed his neck, like he was fighting the urge to pin Riley to the ground and screw her before all his relatives.

Creepy motherfucker, Riley thought, even though the mental image of riding him out in the open did somewhat turn her on.

They traveled deeper into the forest, until the familiar scent of her son assaulted Riley's senses.

"Ryan!" Riley called. "Ryan!"

Riley dashed through the thick foliage to a large clearing where several children and wolves were playing. A group of elderly women looked on from a distance.

"Ryan!" she called again.

A black wolf bounded towards her, jumping straight into Riley's arms and sending her crashing backwards onto the ground.

The wolf enthusiastically licked her face, then transformed into a human child with pale skin and dark hair.

"Mama!" Ryan cried, wrapping his small arms around Riley's neck.

"Ryan," she sobbed and hugged him tightly like he could disappear at any moment. "I missed you."

Joy spread through Riley's body as Ryan's warmth seeped into hers. She ran a hand through his hair.

"Papa! Papa!" Ryan enthusiastically cried and pointed at Elijah.

Don't go to him! Riley wanted to yell, but she held back.

It wouldn't be good to make a scene in front of their son.

"Hey, buddy." Elijah smiled and ruffled Ryan's hair. "Having fun?"

Ryan enthusiastically nodded, transforming back into a wolf and bounding back to the group of children.

Riley felt a pang of loneliness. She finally had him in her arms again, but he was already gone.

"See," said Elijah. "He's happy here."

"That's because he's a child." Riley pulled herself to her feet. "He doesn't know any better."

"He's a werewolf," said Elijah. "He belongs with his own kind."

"But he's also human."

"You're either one or the other, you can't be both."

"Only when it's convenient for you," Riley hissed back.

Elijah sighed, glancing at the elderly women who were watching them with rapt attention. "Look.....Can we talk about this somewhere else? I don't want to fight in front of the elders."

"Fine," Riley snapped, brushing the dirt from her dress.

She blindly walked deeper into the forest, angrily stomping on leaves and stray branches as Elijah followed behind.

He took hold of Riley's wrist and tugged her to face him, pulling her close to his body. "This place is much more suited for werewolf children than that human town."

"That town was our home," said Riley.

"As long as you kept him hidden. Here, he's free to be himself without having to hold back." Elijah gently rubbed Riley's palm with his thumb, causing heat to rise in her cheeks. "You can also be yourself."

Riley pulled her hand out of his grasp. "I am myself."

"No, you're not," said Elijah. "You're still pretending to be human."

"I am human."

"Not anymore. You're a werewolf now. Just like me. Things would be easier if you just accepted it."

Riley ground her teeth. How dare he walk into her life and tell her what to do.

"I know that you feel it too." Elijah reached out, rubbing a finger along her bare upper arm. "This need to be together."

"No, I don't!" Riley snapped.

"Liar. Every time you try to run, you come straight back to my bed."

"That's because....."

Elijah took hold of Riley shoulders, pushing her back against a tree.

"The human you says one thing." He leaned down to press his lips to her ear. "But the wolf you says another." Elijah pressed his warm body against hers, rolling his swollen groin. "The wolf in you is so possessive and demanding. She knows that we need to be together."

"You're so full of shit, Elijah," Riley gasped, but she gave into his touches, letting him hike her leg over his hip so that he could hump her warm center.

"I like it when you pin me down." He pressed a series of warm kisses to her neck. "Riding me until you cum. Human you is so confusing.....but I know that once you transform, you'll come back."

"*Dream on*," Riley whispered, but she wrapped her arms around Elijah's neck, giving into the rapidly growing warmth between her legs.

She was still pissed, but it felt too good to stop. The animal inside her loved it and Riley didn't have the strength to fight back.

Elijah pulled away to undo his jeans and free his swollen cock. He pulled up Riley's dress, then slipped down her panties to slide into her wet heat, letting out a sigh of relief as his dick bottomed out.

Riley hissed and gripped him tightly, burying her head against his neck.

Elijah slowly thrust. "It's okay," he huffed. "I can live like this. Even if you can't let go of your human ideas, we'll be happy together."

"Please shut up," Riley moaned, trying to concentrate on the intoxicating pleasure growing in her core.

Elijah held her tightly as he rolled his hips. "We can live here together.....with Ryan ....and our future children too."

We're not having more children, Riley thought, but they were doing nothing to stop it. They had unprotected sex several times. She could already be pregnant.

"We're both going to be so happy together," said Elijah.

Riley nodded, mostly because she could feel her climax approaching.

Her groin went numb as she reached the point of no return. Riley tightly clung to Elijah and ground her pulsing clit against him.

She gasped as pleasure exploded outwards from her core, reducing her to a trembling mess.

Elijah hissed as her pussy hugged and sucked him deeper. He frantically pounded his hips until he unleashed himself with a moan, spraying his seed deep into her body without any regard for the consequences.

Riley couldn't deny that she loved seeing him cum.

Elijah rested his face against Riley's neck, basking in her warmth as the post orgasm high spread through his limbs.

Riley sighed and ran her hands through his hair, inhaling his masculine scent.

She still didn't trust him, but Riley couldn't see any other options. She would just have to go along with his deluded fantasies until she figured out a way to escape.

CHAPTER FOUR

The days passed in a blur.

Riley spent most of them under Elijah. His fingers threaded through hers as he quietly moved in and out of her body, muttering loving words and promises of more children.

Riley moaned and let him do as he wanted. She passively lay back on the sheets or allowed the wolf inside her to fuck him senseless.

Elijah loved to be held down and dominated.

Riley's alone time was spent wandering around the house, looking for something to do while Elijah was off helping his family.

She prepared Ryan's room, organising the sheets and setting up the bed. She even drew a few simple pictures to decorate the white walls.

Elijah promised that his family would let Ryan come live with them once Riley was mentally stable.

"I'm not crazy," Riley once told Elijah. "I took care of him alone since he was born."

Elijah went silent like he was looking for the right thing to say. "I know… but they don't usually let people live here who used to be human. They think that all human born werewolves are uncontrollable."

Riley huffed and crossed her arms. Several explicit ways of describing his people entered her mind, but she held back.

Riley went to visit Ryan every day, but Ryan soon became distracted by his new friends, wriggling out of her grasp and running off to join them.

Riley sat and watched Ryan play in the forest, but the curious stares of the elders made Riley uncomfortable.

Elijah assured Riley that she was more than welcome, but as soon as he was gone, his people didn't hide that Riley was an outsider.

She heard the elders whisper amongst themselves. They said that she wasn't a *real* werewolf like them. She was a human who was bitten by a stray and could potentially lose her mind.

Riley blocked out their words and pretended that it didn't bother her. She didn't need their friendship or approval. She had no desire to be like them.

Let them say what they want, she thought. *None of it will matter when I'm gone.*

One morning, Ryan dashed across the field towards her holding a white daisy in his open palm. "Flower! Flower" he enthusiastically sang.

Riley wanted to cry. He was finally starting to talk.

"Yes, it's very pretty," Riley said while holding back tears.

Ryan happily passed her the flower, then ran back to rejoin his friends. He laughed as they switched between their human and wolf forms.

Ryan seemed more at ease when he wasn't forced to act human.

Maybe he's better off here, Riley thought to herself, lowering her head so that Ryan wouldn't see the tears running down her face.

Having Ryan stay with the elders relieved Riley's stress. They were far more experienced in raising children than her.

Elijah provided for all her needs, so Riley wasn't forced to work low paying jobs. All she had to do was sit in the house until he came home to fuck her.

As easy as her new life was, Riley couldn't help but feel miserable.

It wasn't bad when Elijah was around, but excruciating loneliness set in the moment he was gone. She had no friends or family in the settlement.

Sometimes she'd just stare out the window for hours, thinking of all the people who she left behind.

Elijah seemed aware of her mood, often silently watching without ever bringing it up.

They didn't talk much. Words were unnecessary between them. There was a strange connection that bound them together through no will of her own.

"I have a surprise for you today," Elijah said one morning while getting dressed.

Riley stopped staring at the wall and sat up to face him, pulling a sheet around her naked body.

"What is it?" she asked.

"Be good for me while I'm gone and you'll see." He leaned down to plant a kiss on her forehead.

Riley rolled her eyes. She wasn't his pet.

Elijah let out a laugh and walked out the room.

Riley tried to pretend that his absence didn't bother her.

Riley showered, got dressed, then wandered the house, looking for Elijah's mysterious *surprise.* Everything was the same as the night before.

She sighed and collapsed on the couch, counting the cracks in the ceiling. There was no T.V or internet, and the few books in the house were full of warped werewolf ideology.

She assumed that having too much knowledge of the outside world would make it harder for the elders to control their people.

There was a knock on the door.

Riley wanted to ignore it. She didn't have the energy to talk with one of the werewolf lemmings, but her curiosity got to her.

Perhaps it had something to do with Elijah's surprise?

Riley got to her feet and went to answer the door.

She undid the lock and turned the handle to find a tall young woman with black braided hair.

"Wanda," Riley gasped.

It was years since she last saw her friend. Wanda helped Riley adjust when she first became a werewolf. They lived together at the academy until Riley left.

Wanda barely looked any different from the last time they parted, but her bright make-up and nail polish was gone, replaced by neutral colors and a faded yellow summer dress.

"Riley!" Wanda cried, dashing forward to embrace Riley. "It's been so long!"

"Where have you been?" asked Riley. "When you stopped replying, I thought that something might have happened to you."

"I'm so sorry about that," said Wanda. "The service out here is horrible, so I didn't bother bringing my phone."

"You've been here the whole time?"

"Yep, moved here soon after I got married." Wanda pulled away to show off a flashy gold ring.

Riley wasn't pleased that her friend had married into a creepy cult, but she put on her best fake smile. "Wow, that's great. Come in. You'll have to tell me more about it."

Riley led Wanda through the house and into the sitting room. "So who's the lucky guy?"

"Romulus." Wanda took a seat on the sofa. "It was all set up by my grandmother. I didn't like him much at first, because he's older than me and already has two wives, but they handle most of the chores, so I can just do what I want."

"Oh..." Riley searched for the right thing to say. "That sounds.....nice...."

"You were right about my old boyfriend Jimmy," said Wanda. "That guy was insane. He chained me in the basement when I tried to break it off."

"Seriously? That must have been terrible, Wanda."

"Nah, it was nothing," Wanda said with a casual wave of her hand. "Happens all the time."

Riley was lost for words. She had forgotten how insane Wanda's life stories could quickly become.

"But enough about me," Wanda said. "You'll have to tell me what you've been up to."

"Well...." Riley wasn't sure how to phrase things without sounding too grim. "Well... I had a son."

"I know! Elijah told me all about it. I saw him with the other children. He's absolutely adorable."

"Thanks." Riley smiled. "Then I went and helped Scott in East Cove for a while....then I came here."

Riley's story was simple and excluded her struggles as a single parent and Elijah abducting them both, but she didn't want to bring down Wanda's bright mood.

"I'm so glad that everything worked out," said Wanda. "I just knew that you and Elijah were meant to be together. You should have seen him while you were gone. He was so grim and miserable."

"Really?"

"Yes," said Wanda. "Latavia was livid because he wouldn't sleep with her, even after the wedding. He mostly just went into the forest and sulked."

There was a strange warmth in Riley's chest. She realized that she was glad to hear that Elijah missed her.

"I knew that he'd never get better unless you came back," said Wanda. "So I told him about you living in East Cove."

Riley forgot to breathe.

"You what?" Riley hoped that she had misheard.

Wanda was oblivious to Riley's shock. "I just knew that things would work out if you came back. And look. You and Elijah are together and-"

"*Get out*," Riley hissed.

"What?" Wanda flinched, smile fading from her face.

"How could you do that to me? You were supposed to be my friend. How could you tell him where I was?"

Wanda's gaze fell to the carpet. She nervously clasped her hands. "I mean....I didn't really have much of a choice....I mean he just kept asking... and he looked so sad... and I really thought-"

"Get out!" Riley snapped, pointing at the door. White hot rage licked at her insides. The need to transform itched under her skin.

If Wanda didn't leave, Riley wasn't sure if she could stop herself from tearing the other woman apart.

"Riley-"

"Get out now!" Riley shouted.

Wanda's shoulders slumped. She stood to her feet and silently left the room, quietly closing the front door behind her.

Riley lashed out at the closest object, a lamp by the sofa. She knocked it to the floor, hoping to see it shatter into a thousand pieces, but it bounced along the carpet, coming to a rest by the opposite sofa.

Riley buried her head in her hands, digging her nails into her scalp.

She couldn't believe that Wanda sold her out.

They were supposed to be friends. Wanda knew how much Riley didn't like werewolf society. If Wanda had only kept her mouth shut, then Riley would still be back in East Cove with Trissy, Vanessa, and Scott.

Scott....

"Shit," Riley swore.

Wanda had Scott's contact details.

Riley cursed herself for not realizing sooner. Scott was the only person she knew who could hook her up with werewolf suppressant medication.

"You idiot," Riley moaned and tugged at her hair, debating whether or not to run after Wanda and beg for help.

There was a knock at the door.

Thinking that Wanda had come back to apologize, Riley got up to answer it.

She quickly turned the door handle and pulled it open. "Wanda, I'm-"

The words died in her throat.

It wasn't Wanda.

Before her stood a thin blond woman in her early forties, dressed in a designer skirt and blouse with her hair tightly pulled back.

Elijah's mother.

Their last meeting five years earlier didn't go well. Seeing her again was enough to make Riley's heart race.

Elijah's mother raked her gaze down Riley's simple dress and disheveled hair. She let out a sigh. "I suppose that will have to do."

Riley wanted to slam the door in the woman's face, but she held back, for Elijah's sake.

"Can I help you?" Riley asked with a strained smile.

"You've been summoned."

"Summoned?"

"By Elijah's grandfather."

Riley swallowed. She was yet to meet the man who Elijah spoke of so highly.

"He sent me to fetch you," said Elijah's mother. "He's eager to meet the woman who holds my dear son's affection," she added with a hint of bitterness.

"Now?"

"Yes, now," Elijah's mother snapped back. "Come on."

Riley sighed and slipped on a pair of sandals, stepping out of the house and closing the door behind her.

She purposely walked a few feet behind Elijah's mother as the older woman led her down the road, past small mansions and expensive cars.

"Don't get any strange ideas," said Elijah's mother. "Just because my deluded son is enamored by you, doesn't mean that the rest of our family feels the same."

Riley rolled her eyes. She expected nothing less from the bitter woman.

"A lifetime of planning all gone to waste," Elijah's mother huffed. "So many relationships ruined because of you."

"Hey," Riley snapped. "I'm only here because your son made me. Shouldn't you be having this conversation with him instead of me."

Elijah's mother stopped and spun on her high heels, glaring daggers at Riley.

"*You stupid, stupid, girl,*" she hissed. "Your pitiful human brain can't comprehend what you've done to my son. It would have been different if he had bonded himself to another werewolf, but instead he has to spend the rest of his life stuck with you, an unstable muncher who will bring him nothing but pain."

"Pain?" Riley laughed. "He's the one who ruined my life."

"And there's the problem," she said. "Your primitive human mind can't accept the wolf. As much as the wolf craves to be with Elijah, your human self constantly rejects him. It will only continue like this, round and around, until the day that you die." Elijah's mother sighed and turned back to the road. "My poor pitiful son," she muttered, then continued on her way.

Riley clenched her teeth and followed.

Deluded bitch, she thought.

Riley was clearly the victim, not Elijah, but she couldn't deny that some of the older woman's words were right.

Riley constantly felt at war with herself. She could see the way that it bothered Elijah. He wanted her to be part of his fated-mates fantasy, but Riley found it impossible to forget her human needs. She refused to blindly trust someone who betrayed her in the past.

They arrived at a large white mansion with several expensive cars parked in the driveway. Two large wooden doors were wide open, leading to a long tiled hallway. The walls were lined with ceramic vases filled with fresh flowers.

"My father-in-law is the leader of this settlement," said Elijah's mother, leading Riley inside to a red wooden door. "Remember that when he's speaking with you."

Riley nodded.

Elijah's mother paused to take a deep breath, then turned the handle and pushed open the door.

Inside was a spacious study filled with bookshelves and antique furniture, but Riley didn't have long to examine the room until her attention was instantly drawn by several sharp cries.

Latavia was fully naked and spread out on a wooden desk, large pregnancy bump fully on display.

Her slim legs were wrapped around a much older man, gasping as he thrust his cock deep inside her.

Riley could only assume that the old man was Elijah's grandfather.

He was younger than she expected, no older than sixty. She could tell from his facial structure that he was related to Elijah. They had the same nose and eyes.

He was fully clothed from the waist up, groaning as he rocked his hips.

Riley quickly averted her gaze to the floor.

Could things get anymore fucked up?

"Just take a seat on the sofa," huffed Elijah's grandfather without losing his rhythm.

Riley remained still, too shocked to move.

Elijah's mother took hold of her shoulders, leading Riley to a leather sofa and gently pushing her down onto the cushions.

Riley glanced at the older woman's face to see hints of discomfort, but Elijah's mother quickly left the room before Riley could examine her any further.

Riley clasped her hands and kept her gaze focused on the carpet, but it was impossible to block out the grunts and gentle moans. The sound of skin slapping together echoed throughout the room.

Latavia let out a small whimper as she came, shuddering against the desk.

Elijah's grandfather followed soon afterwards, unleashing his cum deep inside her pregnant body without bothering to pull out. His wrinkled hands gently squeezed her thighs as he basked in the post orgasm high.

Latavia remained silent and still, until Elijah's grandfather pulled out, allowing her to slide off the desk.

Latavia picked up her clothes, pulling on a tight white dress that barely covered her thighs. It failed to hide the fresh cum running down her bare legs.

Latavia then slipped on a pair of heels and strode past Riley and out the door.

Elijah's grandfather cleaned himself with a small towel, then slipped his cock back into his underwear, readjusting his clothes. His cold blue eyes gazed over Riley.

"My grandson certainly seems enamored by you." He said. "Now that you're here, I can see the appeal."

Riley shuddered.

Who the fuck did he think he was?

Elijah's grandfather took a seat at his desk, resting his hands where Latavia's naked body sat moments earlier.

"We had grand plans for Elijah," he said. "I hoped that he could take other wives and father more children, but that seems impossible now that he's imprinted on you."

"What..." Riley was caught between running and her own curiosity. "What do you mean by *imprinting*?"

"It's an old phenomenon that pops up from time to time." The old man sighed. "When two wolves become unusually attached to each other at first sight. I thought that Elijah's superior breeding would have made him immune, but I was wrong."

"Is there.....any way to stop it?"

Elijah's grandfather coughed like he was suppressing a chuckle. "If there was, you wouldn't be here. My grandson can't even stomach the idea of sleeping with another woman. The rest of us have to pick up the slack."

Is that what you call sleeping with his wife? Riley wanted to ask.

"Now that you're finally here to satisfy his needs," said Elijah's grandfather. "Hopefully he'll live up to some of his former potential."

Riley nodded, hoping that if she just agreed to everything he said, she could leave faster.

"Your inferior breeding makes it difficult for you to understand our ways," said the old man. "But if you keep your head down and do as you're told, then we'll allow you to co-exist beside us. Step out of line and....... My grandson would be devastated if we physically harmed you, but that doesn't mean that we can't chain you to his bed."

Riley nodded, digging her nails into her thighs.

Elijah's grandfather leaned back in his chair. "Your role here is to satisfy his physical needs and birth his children. Another ten would be ideal. Can your weak human body manage that?"

Fuck no, Riley thought.

His words only strengthened her resolve to escape.

Elijah's grandfather wasn't pleased at her silence. "Is there some kind of problem, my dear?"

"No..no..sir," Riley stuttered. "Just thinking.... about all those babies."

Elijah's grandfather nodded. "Your offspring won't be as pure, but they can still be useful for the future......workers to help with our cause."

"Okay, sir."

"If they prove their loyalty, then one day they may enjoy the glorious society that we will build for them."

"Okay, sir."

"It's only a shame that Elijah couldn't have produced more with pure-bred women. I should have kept him here instead of sending him to that school."

"Yes, such a shame." Riley also wished that Elijah had never gone to the academy.

She glanced at the door, wondering when she could escape the old man's crazed ranting.

"Is there somewhere you need to be?" Elijah's grandfather asked.

Riley jolted. "No...I.....I just.... need to go meet Elijah.....he needs me... .for the breeding....and stuff....."

"Oh, yes, go right along," the old man said with a wave of his hand. "I've heard that my grandson can be rather demanding."

"Yes, best not to keep him waiting." Riley quickly got to her feet. "Thanks for the meeting."

Elijah's grandfather didn't say anything. He opened a draw to his desk and pulled out a stack of papers like Riley was already gone.

Riley quickly walked out of the room and down the hall, clenching her fists.

It was difficult to decide who was the most fucked up person. Elijah's mother, Latavia, or his grandfather?

No wonder Elijah was so deluded.

CHAPTER FIVE

Riley was glad to find Elijah waiting in the kitchen. It saved her from having to hunt him down.

Elijah's mouth curved up into an excited smile, but it didn't ease her anger.

"Your grandfather and wife are fucking," she said.

Riley expected to catch Elijah off guard, but he didn't even flinch.

"Oh....Did Latavia tell you?" he asked.

"No." Riley was shocked at his calm demeanor. "He just invited me to watch him screw her on his desk."

"Well.... Grandfather is a busy man. He often schedules meetings close together."

Riley sighed and crossed her arms. Elijah was unbelievable. He was completely used to weird shit. "So you don't care that your grandfather is screwing your wife?"

Elijah shook his head. "I told you before. Latavia and I are only married in name, so she's free to be with who she wants."

"Even when she's pregnant?"

"Latavia's been pregnant plenty of times before. I'm sure that she knows what she can and can't do."

Riley was lost for words. Was there anything that could unnerve him?

"What if I'm next?" she asked. "What if he tries to get in my pants?"

"He wouldn't do that." Elijah stepped forward to take hold of Riley's upper arms. "He knows that we're fated mates, so no one here will touch you."

"How do you know that?"

"Because you have me." He wrapped his arms around Riley's back to pull her close. "I won't let anything happen to you."

Elijah seemed sure of himself, but Riley doubted that he could fully protect her from his world.

"Why don't we leave?" asked Riley. "We could go somewhere far away where none of them will find us."

"I can't do that."

"Why not?"

"My family needs me."

"They'll live without you."

"No." He shook his head. "I can't do that."

Riley sighed. She wasn't surprised. He was still the same loyal drone who couldn't comprehend going against his elders.

Elijah gripped her tighter. "We can build our own world for ourselves here. Just you and me."

"Whatever," Riley muttered, pressing her face to his chest to take in his scent.

As annoying as he could be, Elijah's affection was endearing. He genuinely seemed to love her, no matter how fucked up his reasoning was.

Riley didn't believe in fated mates, but it felt nice to give into the fantasy, if only for a moment.

The wolf inside her purred as Riley relinquished control.

"It's okay," Elijah murmured and buried his face in her hair. "Just give in."

Riley emptied her mind, giving into the animal inside.

She stepped back, pulling her thin dress over her head. It fell to the floor, followed by her bra and underwear.

Elijah silently watched.

Riley abandoned her human form, shifting into her grey wolf self. She dashed down the hallway and out of the house.

Elijah's footsteps pounded behind her. He stripped his clothes, then transformed into a large white wolf.

The woods called to Riley. She dashed straight into the foliage, immersing herself in the sights and smells.

It was where she felt most at ease. It was where she belonged.

All frivolous human things were irrelevant to *the wolf.*

She could hear Elijah gaining on her, but Riley didn't relent, bounding over bushes and fallen tree branches.

If he wanted to catch her, he would have to work for it.

His large body crashed into hers, pinning Riley to the damp grass. His thick cock thrust inside her as his sharp teeth clamped down on her neck.

Riley wasn't sure if they were wolves or humans, all that mattered was feeling him deep inside her.

She never wanted to be alone again.

Elijah pumped his hips in a frenzy, giving into the primal urges pulsing through his brain. He muttered promises of devotion and children, lacing his fingers with Riley's and pressing their hands together.

The wolf inside her hummed.

Riley moaned and closed her eyes, savoring the sensations flowing through her lower body. She angled her hips to get more friction against her clit, gasping as she was hit by a strong wave of pleasure.

Elijah hissed.

He ripped his cock out and pressed his mouth to Riley's groin, frantically licking her slit.

Riley gripped his hair, rolling her hips into his mouth as overwhelming pressure grew in her lower body.

It felt heavenly. Pure happiness rolled through her in waves.

Riley jolted as she came, gasping and shaking as Elijah worked her through the orgasm.

He climbed back over her body, sliding his pulsing erection straight into her soaked entrance, groaning in bliss.

"I'll protect you," he hissed with a roll of his hips. "No matter what happens...... I'll protect you."

Riley nodded. He looked so beautiful.

Elijah came with a groan, pumping his hips until every drop of cum flowed deep inside her.

Riley hugged him tightly until his breathing returned to normal.

Perhaps it wouldn't be so bad, she thought to herself. *To try living in his fantasy world.*

Riley had no other option until she found a way to escape.

CHAPTER SIX

Elijah's car curved around a narrow mountain road, past rows of large trees that blocked out rays from the setting sun.

Riley's heart skipped a beat every time that they turned a tight bend, terrified that the car would plunge into the thick undergrowth.

Elijah threaded his fingers through hers, bringing Riley's hand to his lips, lightly pressing a kiss.

Riley's groin tingled with anticipation, but Elijah's gaze was firmly focused on the dirt road.

"Later," he murmured, like he could smell her need.

They soon caught up to a convoy of cars that were traveling up the mountain. One by one, they parked in a large field close to the summit.

There were mostly young people from the settlement, but there were also other werewolves that Riley had never seen before.

Elijah turned off the engine and got out of the car, undoing his buttons and stripping off his shirt.

He wasn't the only one. The surrounding people were also casually removing their clothes.

Shit, Riley swore and averted her gaze to the ground. She'd forgotten how casual werewolves all were about stripping.

"What's wrong?" Elijah asked.

"*Why is everyone naked?*" Riley hissed.

"The road ends here, so we need to transform to go the rest of the way."

"But can't we just walk?"

Elijah blinked like he'd never thought of it.

"Hey, Elijah!" called a tall naked man covered in blond hair. He walked over and casually patted Elijah on the shoulder, but Riley couldn't avoid getting an eyeful of his dong. "Grandfather says that he wants you up front."

Elijah looked towards Riley as though asking for permission.

"It's okay," Riley said with a strained smile. "I'll catch up later."

"Sorry," said Elijah as his body began to transform. "I'll find you later."

He shifted into his wolf form, disappearing into the dark woods along with the other wolves.

Riley let out a sigh. She didn't want to be there, but the event seemed important to Elijah.

She was trying to be a better partner. Hoping that she could find a way of easing her loneliness through him.

She doubted that going along with his insanity was the answer, but it didn't hurt to try.

"Riley!" cried a voice behind her.

Riley turned to see a young naked woman dashing towards her.

Her long red hair did little to hide her bouncing breasts. She launched herself at Riley, embracing her in a tight hug.

Riley was too confused to move.

"It's been ages," said the woman with a brilliant smile. "I never thought that I'd see you here."

The woman seemed vaguely familiar, but Riley couldn't place her.

The red haired woman let go of Riley and took a step back. "It's me, Heather...you know.....from the academy."

"Oh," said Riley. The name brought back memories of a younger Heather who once helped Riley find herbs in the forest. "How have you been?"

"Great," said Heather. "Just busy doing my part for the cause, you know. Managed to pop out twins last spring."

"Wow...that's great." Riley tried to keep her gaze on Heather's face. "You look great."

"Right," Heather said. "You'd never think that I've had seven so far."

"Seven?" Riley gasped. She was certain that Heather wasn't much older than her.

"You'd think that would be enough to please father," Heather sighed. "But he's always bugging me for more. He's been pressuring me to come here since I gave birth."

"Oh..." said Riley. "That must be terrible."

"You have no idea," Heather moaned, glancing up at the darkening sky. "It should be starting soon. You should transform."

"I..I ..think I'll just walk," said Riley. She had no desire to get naked in front of everyone.

"Okay," said Heather. "I'll walk with you."

Heather linked arms with Riley, leading her to a path buried amongst the trees.

Riley flinched, but she had no idea where to go, so she didn't pull away.

"So.....what kind of event is this?" Riley asked.

"Just a little get together we all have once a month," said Heather. "A lot of people from nearby clans usually come."

"Like a meeting?"

"Yeah.....you could say that. One of the elders usually does some talking."

Riley nodded. It sounded dull. No wonder Elijah was so vague about it.

They walked through the darkness, brushing past thick bushes and branches. Several wolves bounded past them as the beating of drums echoed in the distance.

Heather and Riley emerged into a large open clearing. There were several small bonfires as groups of men and women silently looked towards the top of the mountain.

They were all stark naked, but there were several men with red and white paint smeared across their bare chests.

"*Those are the old ones,*" Heather whispered. "They live out in the forest and act more like wolves than humans. It took a lot of work for the elders to make them come."

A muscular man with a fur pelt draped over his shoulders curiously cocked his head in Riley's direction, gazing over her clothes.

Riley didn't feel malice. More like he had never seen someone like her.

The screech of a microphone echoed around them.

There was a rock formation on the other side of the clearing. It had been converted into a stage with large speakers and bright lights.

Elijah's grandfather stood in the center, dressed in an assortment of animal furs. He wore a headdress made from colorful feathers that made him appear taller.

Elijah and Latavia stood behind him.

Latavia's arms were crossed over her chest like she could barely stomach standing next to her husband. Her bare stomach was more prominent than before.

Elijah looked equally uncomfortable, but he placed a hand on her lower back and smiled towards the crowd.

There was a group of small children standing beside them.

Riley didn't think much of it, until she scanned their pale faces to see a resemblance to Elijah.

They were his children.

They didn't even look at their mother or father, instead fidgeting or staring off into the distance like their own parents were strangers. The oldest one looked at least ten. Elijah would have been about fifteen when he was conceived.

Riley wanted to throw up. The youngest didn't look much older than Ryan.

There were several other pale men and women on the stage, but Riley was too mortified to pay them any attention.

Elijah's grandfather raised his arms towards the audience. "Brothers, sisters." His deep voice echoed amongst the hills. "For too long we have lived in the shadows of *them,* condemned to the outskirts as *they* drive the planet into ruin."

The crowd silently watched, eating up every word.

"I come before you to propose a way out of our subservient existence," Elijah's grandfather continued. "The slow death of the human race, gives us an opportunity to reproduce and outgrow them. Only through large numbers will we gain the power to take what is ours."

Several members of the crowd raised their arms and cheered.

"To achieve our dreams, we must copulate and breed. Every pregnancy is a gift. Every child you create is another soldier for our cause. Only through your hard work, will we gain the power to defeat mankind!"

"He can't be fucking serious," Riley muttered, turning to Heather, but the other woman was enthralled by the old man's words.

Not her too, Riley thought, but no one around them seemed to show any disapproval.

"Go, my brothers and sisters!" Elijah's grandfather boomed. "Breed for your future. Your children's future. And for all wolf kind!"

The crowd cheered. The beating of drums played through the speakers.

All around Riley, the people started to dance, pressing their naked bodies together without a hint of shame.

They rubbed and licked at each other's skin, sliding hands between legs to stimulate sensitive areas.

It wasn't long before they were fucking, riding each other without saying a word.

A large red haired man slipped an arm around Heather's waist, rubbing his erection against her arse before slipping straight into her wet heat, thrusting in and out as Heather gasped.

Heather didn't even look at his face, happily accepting his dick as she trembled and groaned.

Riley was speechless. They were merrily screwing only inches away.

Heather slipped a hand between her thighs to rub her clit. "So good," she gasped. "Put lots of strong babies inside me."

It was like Riley wasn't there.

A guy old enough to be Riley's father, winked and walked towards her, erection swinging between his thighs, but Riley quickly turned her back and stormed away.

"Fuck this shit," she muttered.

She couldn't believe that Elijah dragged her to another fucked up werewolf orgy.

She was going to go wait in the car.

A large arm wrapped around Riley's waist.

"*There you are*," Elijah whispered in her ear.

"Fuck off, Elijah," Riley hissed, struggling out of his grip.

"Still so shy," Elijah laughed, refusing to let her go. "Just relax."

"I'm not going to be part of this fuckfest."

"But the only one fucking you will be me," Elijah hummed, biting down on Riley's ear.

Riley shuddered as a jolt of pleasure rocked through her core.

Elijah's erection rubbed against her back as he pressed his warm naked body against her. His large fingers wrapped around her breast, gently squeezing it as he licked her earlobe.

"Magnificent, isn't it," Elijah hummed while watching the scene before them. "So many tribes all coming together."

"That's one way of putting it," Riley gasped.

A familiar heat pooled in her groin. The wolf inside Riley stirred, clawing its way to the surface.

If Riley tried to run, she knew that it would take over and come back. The stupid animal wouldn't pass up an opportunity to get laid.

Elijah rolled his cock against Riley's soft arse, letting out a groan. His fingers crept up her thigh before slipping into her underwear, rubbing back and forth along Riley's slit.

She jolted against his touch.

"Just look at them all," Elijah whispered, pressing kisses along her neck. "All doing what they were born to."

Riley moaned and relaxed against him, giving into the intoxicating pleasure rapidly growing between her legs.

She glanced up to watch everyone breeding like mindless animals. If one man finished with a woman, another would soon take his place. Several couples readily switched partners like it was the most natural thing in the world.

Riley gasped.

Was she fucked up if watching people screw turned her on?

"I knew that you'd like it." Elijah's fingers circled her pulsing clit. "You always liked it."

Riley shuddered and gripped his arm, trying her best to remain standing. Overwhelming pressure grew in her groin until it suddenly burst, reducing Riley to a trembling mess as waves of sensation pulsed from her center.

"That's it," Elijah whispered while diligently rubbing her through the orgasm. "Let it all out."

Riley pushed his hand away once it was too much. She turned to face Elijah, wrapping her arms around his neck and crushing their lips together.

Perhaps it was the orgasm speaking, but Riley craved his intimacy. She tugged on his hair as her tongue twined with his.

Elijah groaned, squeezing Riley's arse as his hard cock pressed against her stomach. He took hold of her dress, urgently tugging it over Riley's head.

Riley stepped back to help him, removing her clothes along with her underwear, until she was just as naked as everyone else.

"I want them to see," Elijah hummed while littering Riley's face in kisses. "How beautiful you look when my cock's deep inside you."

Riley laughed, mind warm and fuzzy from the post orgasm high.

"On your knees," Elijah ordered.

Riley did as he asked, getting on her hands and knees like a dog, spreading her legs wide in preparation for his shaft.

Elijah knelt behind her, grabbing hold of Riley's thighs and rubbing his thick dick along her drenched slit, coating himself in her fluids.

The moans and cries of several climaxes echoed around them.

Elijah's cock caught on Riley's entrance. He pressed in, bottoming out with several small thrusts.

Riley gripped the grass beneath her palms. The feeling of him buried deep inside her was enough to make her groin pulse with need.

Elijah hissed and rolled his hips, savoring the sensation of her warm wet body hugging his sensitive dick.

"Do you see?" He groaned. "How wonderful things can be?"

Riley didn't answer, rocking back against his groin to encourage him to speed up.

Elijah pounded into her body in time with the drums, balls slapping against her arse with every strong thrust.

Riley closed her eyes, enjoying the sensations pulsing through her core.

Her human mind screamed that the massive orgy was fucked up, but the wolf inside her loved every second.

Riley cried out every time that Elijah's cock slammed into her cervix.

"Fuck," huffed Elijah. "I love it when you're loud."

He sped up his pace as he reached the point of no return, drilling deep into her warmth until he unleashed himself with a roar, spraying wave after wave of cum deep into her fertile womb.

Riley couldn't deny that she loved every second.

Elijah pulled out once he was through, causing his seed to trickle down Riley's naked thighs.

He pushed Riley back against the grass and onto her back, burying his face between her legs. His hot mouth wrapped around her swollen clit, licking and sucking like a man possessed.

Riley gasped and ran a hand through his hair, pushing him closer as pure joy bloomed from her center.

It was magical.

Riley gazed up at the stars as she soared towards climax, gasping and shaking as she came.

Riley knew that a harsh reality was waiting for her when they returned home, but she allowed herself to enjoy that one moment of pleasure.

CHAPTER SEVEN

The midnight orgy made Riley realize that the werewolf settlement was more fucked up than she could have possibly imagined.

It was impossible to see the people the same way as before.

Riley sat on a hill, basking in the midday sun as two teenage girls sat giggling on a picnic blanket nearby, showing off their swollen stomachs.

"I hope it's a boy," one said. "I've already got two girls."

"Fat chance," laughed the other. "Jerry's only fathered girls so far. I told you that you should have screwed Isaac more."

"But he always wants to cum on my face. It's so gross."

"Not as bad as Harry. I heard that he tries to stick it in the bum."

"That's just like Aaron, except Sasha said that he wanted her to lick it afterwards."

"Ewww, that's so gross!"

Riley listened as the two girls laughed about the local boys strange sex kinks. She doubted that they had ever heard of birth control.

There was a third girl who had been lured away by a guy with a shaved head. She lay back on the grass as he pounded her pussy, naked lower bodies proudly on display.

None of them looked older than twenty.

If they lived on the outside, they'd be in high school or college, but instead they were too busy breeding soldiers for the *cause.*

Riley cursed herself for taking so long to figure it out.

The settlement was a baby farm. The elders encouraged the young adults to have as much sex as possible, then whisked the children away soon after they were born. It freed up the women to fall pregnant again sooner.

It was just like the academy.

Nobody seemed to question the system or the elders' goals. They whole-heartedly believed whatever the bastards told them.

Riley groaned and buried her face in her hands. She found it difficult to sleep at night. By doing nothing and fucking around with Elijah, she'd become part of their insane plot.

Riley thought of burning the whole settlement to the ground, but most of the inhabitants were still children. Even if they were breeding an army of soldiers, they didn't deserve to die.

She also had something else holding her back.

Riley was hit by a familiar wave of nausea.

She didn't bother to fight it, getting to her feet and emptying her stomach into a nearby bush, coughing and hacking until the feeling passed.

Morning sickness was a bitch.

Riley had been through it once when she was pregnant with Ryan. The symptoms were so obvious that it was impossible to lie to herself.

She was pregnant again.

Riley cursed herself for not getting an IUD when she was on the outside, but she didn't plan on Elijah showing up to seduce her inner wolf.

All the stupid animal wanted to do was get knocked up and pump out as many babies as possible. It didn't care if they grew up to destroy human society.

Perhaps she was just as fucked up as everyone else.

Riley wiped her mouth with her sleeve and waited for the nausea to pass.

She was hesitant to tell Elijah about the pregnancy. She didn't want to watch him get excited about a baby that she was still coming to terms with.

There was a woman with dark braided hair walking in the distance, moving along a gravel path through the trees.

There was only one person in the settlement that Riley had seen with that hair.

"Wanda!" Riley called out as she dashed down the hill towards her friend.

Wanda was unnaturally forgiving. Riley hoped that it would work to her advantage.

Wanda spun to face Riley. She was wearing a long orange dress that covered most of her skin.

"Oh, hey Riley," Wanda smiled like Riley had never screamed in her face. "How's it going?"

"Good." The world spun before Riley, but she held back the urge to puke. "I want to apologize for the other day."

"Don't worry about it," Wanda said with a casual wave of her hand. "I was obviously in the wrong."

Fuck yeah, you were, Riley thought.

"It's okay," said Riley. "I know that Elijah can be very....persuasive."

Wanda's shoulders sagged with relief. "They all are...out here...especially towards me, because I'm an outsider."

Riley would have felt more sympathy if she wasn't still pissed. "That sounds.... tough."

"Especially the elders." Wanda glanced over her shoulder. "They have their own way of doing things."

Riley took hold of Wanda's upper arm, gently leading her into the trees. "There's actually something that I wanted to ask you."

"Sure," said Wanda. "Fire away."

"I was wondering..." Riley lowered her voice to a whisper. "*If you have Scott's contact info.*"

"Sure, I guess that it's back in my father's house somewhere...why?"

"I need more of those pills for human werewolves."

Wanda nervously glanced at her feet. "They don't really approve of those here."

"But I wasn't born a werewolf like you. It's difficult for me to cope without them."

"I want to help you...but there are rules."

"No one has to know."

"Elijah would know."

"How?"

"He'll smell it."

"But I'll be gone before he can tell."

Wanda's mouth dropped open in horror. "You're gonna run away, again?"

"Of course. This place is a madhouse. I don't know how you can stand it."

"But I thought the two of you were happy?"

"We are...kinda....but I can be happy again without him if I could get some of those pills."

"Sorry Riley...I really don't want to risk it."

"But I thought you were my friend."

"I am...but I'm also one of the clan now. I need to follow the rules."

"Seriously?" Riley laughed. "You think that you're one of them? The leaders here don't give a shit about you."

Wanda went silent like Riley had slapped her in the face. Her hands clenched into fists. "Well.... we all can't be human loners like you....." Wanda snapped. "I'm just trying to create a better life for myself."

"With a bunch of werewolf white supremacists?"

"It's better to be on the winning side. It will pay off once the war starts."

"Not you too." Riley shook her head. "Don't tell me that you also believe in their bullshit war against humanity?"

"Why not? What has humanity ever done for me?"

Riley struggled to think of a reply.

Wanda may have been her best friend at the academy, but Riley knew little about the other woman's life.

"You were born human, so it's easy for you to live amongst them," Wanda said. "But the rest of us had to spend our whole lives hiding what we truly are."

"And what's that?"

"A better race."

Riley was lost for words.

Wanda had clearly fallen for their ideology, hook, line and sinker.

She couldn't be trusted.

"You're so lucky to be here, Riley," said Wanda. "So many people would kill to be part of this place."

"Well... those people aren't me," said Riley. "Anyone who believes in this bullshit is just going to end up dead."

"Spoken like a non-believer."

"What the fuck does that mean?"

"You'll see," Wanda said with a smug grin.

Riley shook her head. Their relationship years earlier consisted mostly of Wanda listening to Riley's problems and helping her through the werewolf change. Riley never asked Wanda about her ideological beliefs.

Perhaps Wanda had been this way from the very beginning?

"Well....have fun with your little werewolf race war," Riley snapped. "Don't come crying to me when it all blows up in your face!"

"I won't have to," said Wanda. "Because you'll be right there beside us."

"You're unbelievable," Riley muttered.

She spun on her heels and made her way back to the path.

"You'll see!" Wanda yelled back. "Our way is the right way!"

Riley's hands shook with rage. She was too angry to speak.

Riley thought Wanda genuinely wanted to help her years earlier, but perhaps Riley was nothing more than a new recruit for the cause.

Riley was a fool for not seeing it sooner.

Riley stormed back into her house, slamming the door behind her. She was caught between screaming and crying.

Without Wanda, her escape plan was back to square one. There was no way that she could leave Elijah without the medication to control her werewolf urges.

Riley collapsed on the sofa, focusing all her rage at the wall, until she allowed herself to break down.

Weeks of stress and anguish crashed over Riley as tears poured down her face.

"Riley?" echoed Elijah's voice from the second floor.

Riley quickly wiped her face. She didn't want him to see her upset.

"Oh, Riley." Elijah entered the room and sat beside her on the sofa, gathering her up into his arms. "What's wrong?"

"It's nothing." Riley's voice hitched as she tried to pull herself together. "I don't know what came over me."

"Is it because of the baby?"

Riley's insides froze. "How...How do you know?"

"Your scent is different." He gently ran a hand through her hair. "It reminds me of when Latavia's pregnant."

That was enough to make Riley break down again, sobbing against Elijah's sweater.

Of course he was an expert on pregnant women after fathering so many children.

"It's okay." He held Riley close while rubbing her back. "I know that the hormones can make women emotional."

"I don't want to be here anymore," Riley sobbed.

Elijah tightened his grip. "What do you mean?"

"I want to live somewhere else. Can we please just go live somewhere else?"

"Like another settlement?"

"No." Riley shook her head. "Somewhere far away from any were-wolves."

Elijah let out a sigh. "You know that we can't do that."

"Why not?"

"Grandfather needs me here."

"No, he doesn't. He can find another sucker to replace you."

"It's already been decided."

"Why?"

"Because he trusts me the most."

"Only because you roll over and do whatever he wants," Riley snapped.

Elijah shook his head. "Grandfather said that you might be like this.

Many new people have trouble adjusting, but once you get used to being here-"

"I've been here long enough. I've seen enough!"

Elijah pulled away. "Please try...just a little longer... for me."

Riley crossed her arms. It was hard to argue with him when he looked like a kicked puppy, but she couldn't change the way she felt.

"Please," Elijah begged, sliding off the couch and getting on his knees before her. "Just for a little longer....."

"Elijah-"

"*Shhhh*," he hushed. "I just want to make you feel better."

He rolled up Riley's dress and took hold of her underwear, pulling it down her legs and dropping it to the floor. He pried her thighs apart and pressed his mouth to her apex, taking a long swipe with his tongue.

Riley shuddered, relishing in the wet heat against her most sensitive area. She did want to feel better, even for a short moment.

Elijah's tongue circled her clit as he rubbed his growing erection through his pants. His tongue slipped into Riley's entrance, enthusiastically lapping up her fluids.

Riley hissed and closed her eyes, relaxing back against the sofa. He was desperate and eager to please. It was easy to forget her problems when his warm lips were pressed against her.

Elijah undid his zipper and pulled out his throbbing cock, slowly massaging it with one hand as the other gripped Riley's thigh.

Riley ran her hands through his soft hair, pulling his head closer as she rolled her hips against his mouth, chasing her own pleasure.

All that mattered was reaching the end.

Delicious pressure grew in her core until it exploded, reducing Riley to a trembling mess as she tightly gripped Elijah's hair.

He licked her through the orgasm until Riley pushed him away.

Elijah got to his feet, pumping his throbbing erection as he stared at her naked lower half, breathing heavily as he pleasured himself.

Riley watched transfixed.

He came moments later, spraying his seed over Riley's naked groin and thighs.

Riley didn't think that watching Elijah cum on her would be so hot.

Elijah went to the side table and gathered a wad of tissues, wiping Riley's skin clean, then depositing them in the waste paper basket.

He sat on the sofa beside Riley, gathering her up into his arms.

"Just you wait," Elijah murmured against her hair. "Everything will get better."

No it won't, Riley thought, but she didn't want to ruin the moment.

CHAPTER EIGHT

It was empty.

There were no signs of life inside the house where Ryan was staying.

The front door was wide open. It swung on its hinges, banging against the wall with every strong breeze.

There were toys scattered across the living room and the wardrobes were wide open. Children's clothing had been pulled out and tossed on the beds.

"Ryan!" Riley called while making her way through the empty halls. "Ryan!"

She could smell hints of her son, but it was faint, like he hadn't been there in days.

"Ryan!" Riley cried out again.

A week earlier there had been a dozen children and an elderly couple. Ryan seemed happy. Elijah assured her that he'd be safe.

She was an idiot for believing any of them.

"*Fuck*," Riley hissed and anxiously tugged on her hair, heart racing a million miles an hour.

It was all her fault.

She'd put off visiting Ryan after she felt pregnant. She didn't know how to talk to him about the baby and he seemed happy enough with the other children. She assumed it would be fine if she didn't visit for a few days.

She'd paid the price.

Riley dashed out of the house, searching for any sign of Ryan's scent, but there was nothing.

"Hey!" Riley grabbed the shoulders of the first person who walked past, a young teenage girl with blond hair. "Do you know where the people in this house went?"

The girl's face contorted in fear as Riley's panicked fingers dug into her shoulders.

"I....I..don't know..." she stuttered. "They could have moved or something."

"Are you sure? Do you have any idea where they could be?"

"I'm sorry." The girl shook with fear. "I really don't know anything."

She was too terrified to be lying.

Riley released her grip. The girl dashed away.

Without thinking, Riley's body contorted and changed, ripping through her dress and taking the form of a grey werewolf.

She dashed through the forest towards Elijah's scent, shoving open the front door to their home and leaping inside. Riley raced down the hall and through the back door into the garden, seamlessly transforming into her human form.

Elijah was hanging their laundry out to dry on a clothesline. He turned to face Riley the moment she appeared.

"Where's Ryan?" Riley asked.

Elijah glanced down at the basket of wet clothes, but he didn't look surprised, like he knew that the conversation was coming.

"Elijah?" Riley's voice trembled.

Elijah put down the shirt in his hand and walked towards her, pulling Riley into a tight hug.

"It's for the best," he said. "The other settlements are better at taking care of children who grew up with humans."

"Where's Ryan?" Riley asked, struggling out of his hold.

"Somewhere where they can take better care of him. Grandfather said that he'd let me know when-"

Riley tore herself from his grip. She leaped up the stairs and made her way to their room, pulling a dress from the closet.

Elijah appeared moments later. "Where are you going?" he asked, nervously wringing his hands.

"To talk to your grandfather," Riley snapped back. "Or maybe he's actually your father... or uncle.... who the fuck knows in this place."

Elijah nodded like such talk wasn't new. "Good luck," he mumbled.

"Thanks," Riley slipped on the dress, then stormed out of the room. "At least one of us has the balls to stand up to that arsehole."

Nobody stopped Riley as she made her way through Elijah's grandfather's mansion. Pissed off young women stomping through the halls was obviously nothing new.

Riley shoved open the door to the old man's study without knocking.

Elijah's grandfather sat at his desk. A young blond woman was sitting on his lap. The buttons of her blouse were undone as the old man massaged her naked breasts.

She let out a cry of surprise as Riley entered.

Riley was too angry to give a shit about who the old man was fucking.

"Where's my son?" she snapped.

Elijah's grandfather removed his hands from the young woman's chest, pushing her off his lap. "Sandy, dear, can you wait outside?"

The young woman nodded and hastily did up her blouse, quietly walking out of the room and closing the door behind her.

Elijah's grandfather clasped his hands together and looked straight at Riley, letting out a sigh.

"Rebecca, was it?" he asked.

"It's Riley."

"Riley then," the old man said like he had no intention of remembering. "What can I do for you?"

"You can tell me where you took my son."

"And why would I do that?"

"Because he's my son, you dickhead."

Riley focused all her rage into those words, but the old man just looked at her like he was dealing with a disobedient child.

"It came to my attention that your boy was consuming too much of your time. Aren't things better now that you don't have to worry about him?"

It felt like a slap to Riley's face. For too long she had wondered about her life without children, but now that it was happening, she felt nothing but terror.

"No...." Riley's voice hitched. "He's my son."

"Who was clearly holding you back from making more children. Now that he's gone, you'll have plenty of time to make more."

"I'm already pregnant, you dipshit."

"Oh." Elijah's grandfather tapped his fingers against the desk. "Well.... Now you'll have plenty of time to rest."

"Bring him back." Riley's face felt numb, but she held back the tears. "Bring him back now."

"I'm afraid it's too late," the old man shrugged. "It's out of my hands."

"Liar!" she spat. "Where did you take him?"

"To another settlement that's better at raising half-breeds. He belongs with his own kind."

"And where's that?"

"Somewhere that you don't need to worry about, my dear. Your role is to spread your legs and keep my grandson happy. Not go parading through the mountains searching for half-breeds."

Riley's hands shook with rage. She wanted to bound over the desk and strangle the old man.

"Elijah won't like this!" she hissed.

The old man let out a laugh. "Elijah is a good boy who will do what he's told. He understands his place here, unlike you." The old man got to his feet, walking around the desk to face Riley. "We only tolerate your existence because my grandson won't fuck anyone else. If it were up to me, I would have dumped you on the side of the road weeks ago."

He was a foot taller than Riley. She fought the urge to flinch away.

"I won't remove you," the old man continued. "But I can control your life here. I can have you chained to a bed and have every child ripped from your arms the moment that they leave your womb. Don't forget that your only purpose here is to be a warm hole for my grandson's cock."

"Elijah would never let that happen."

"Yes, he would. Because unlike you, Elijah understands his place."

Riley wanted to say that he was bluffing, but she wasn't sure. Elijah was gullible enough to believe all the crap he'd been told. She had no idea what his limit was.

"Are you going to be a good little girl," said the old man. "Or will I have to get out my chains?"

Riley bit her lower lip. She wanted to scream back and claw off his face, but it wouldn't help her get what she wanted.

Riley had to bide her time until she found another way to find Ryan.

She reluctantly nodded.

"Good." Elijah's grandfather took a seat at his desk. "Now go home and spread your legs," he said with a casual wave of his hand. "That boy could do with some stress relief after having to endure a mouthy bitch like you."

Riley ground her teeth and turned to leave, forcing herself to take one step in front of the other.

"And tell Sandy to come back in while you're there." Elijah's grandfather reached down to unzip his pants. "We're not finished yet."

Elijah embraced Riley the moment that she walked through the door, hugging her tightly to his chest.

"I'm so sorry," he said. "I told grandfather you wouldn't like it, but he said that Ryan would be better off with other children who are part human."

Riley felt numb. "Why didn't you tell me?"

"I didn't want to worry you, especially when you're pregnant. I'm sure it's only temporary. He'll probably come back in a year or two."

"A year?" Riley pulled herself out of Elijah's grasp. "He's only four! He'll forget me after a year."

"No, he won't. You're his mother."

"How could you allow this to happen, Elijah?"

"But it happens all the time. My cousins and I often moved between elders."

"When you were four?"

"Yeah, I didn't see my parents much until I was older."

Riley crossed her arms. So much about Elijah finally made sense.

No wonder he was so blindly devoted to the elders and terrified of disappointing his family.

They had fucked him up as well.

"Do you know where they took him?" Riley asked.

"No, but I can ask around."

"Then we can go find him."

Elijah remained silent.

Riley's heart raced in her chest. "We'll go find him, right Elijah?"

Elijah's gaze fell to the carpet. "That's not something that we can do...without permission."

"Bullshit," she spat. "They can't control you like that!"

Elijah let out a sigh of frustration. "Look...it might be hard for you to understand...but there are rules here."

"And?"

"People who go against the elders get exiled."

"But he's your son!"

"I'd never be able to see my parents and other children again! I'm not like you...I can't just do whatever I want when I feel like it."

Riley balled her hands into fists. She was tired of having the same conversation with him again and again. "Can you stop being a fucking lemming for one second and do the right thing?"

"Look..." Elijah wrung his hands with frustration. "I'll try and find another way. I'll talk to Grandfather... or Mother.. maybe one of them can help...we can sort this out without doing anything to upset the elders."

"I don't believe you."

"Can you please trust me....just this one time... I promise that everything will work out."

"That's what you always say."

"Because it's true." He wrapped his arms around Riley's shoulders and pulled her close.

Riley was too tired to fight him, allowing his large fingers to run through her hair.

No matter how many times she tried to reason with him, the answer was always the same. No matter how many times she tried to run, her inner wolf would always come back.

But there was one way that she could leave Elijah forever and go find her son.

If Elijah was dead.

If Riley killed him, perhaps it would be enough to break the bond between them and allow her to leave.

"Everything will be okay," Elijah murmured against her hair. "I promise."

"Yeah," Riley wearily replied. "It will."

CHAPTER NINE

Elijah looked peaceful when he slept.

The lines around his eyes were fainter and his size was less intimidating.

He was a handsome man. Riley would have been proud to have him as her boyfriend if his family weren't insane.

She'd come to accept that there was nothing that she could do to change it. There were hundreds of them, and only one of her.

A large kitchen knife trembled in Riley's hand. It gleamed in the dark room.

All she needed to do was walk across the bedroom and slit Elijah's throat. He'd bleed out on the sheets in seconds and then she'd be free.

Riley wasn't sure if her inner wolf would react well to Elijah's death, but it was her only chance at escaping the bond.

So why was it so fucking hard?

Riley remained frozen by the door, failing to suppress the overwhelming despair at the thought of Elijah's death.

As much as she wanted to leave the settlement and find her son, the thought of watching Elijah choke on his own blood was mortifying.

"*Fuck*," Riley hissed and slipped out of the room.

She walked into the kitchen, slamming the knife back on the counter.

No matter how many times she tried, it was always the same. She found it impossible to kill him.

He was just another pathetic pawn in the cult's screwed up cause. He didn't deserve to die by his lover's hands.

Riley was too frustrated to sleep. She quietly put on her shoes and walked out the front door, making her way to the woods. The cool night air was usually enough to calm her nerves.

She was four months pregnant. The morning sickness had finished and she was starting to show. It wouldn't be much longer before she'd feel the baby move.

Despite all the weak promises, Elijah had yet to track down Ryan. She didn't know if he was even trying, instead just blindly accepting whatever his grandfather wanted him to know.

Maybe the next baby can live with us, was Elijah's latest excuse, like he'd already given up.

Riley walked to the clearing and sat down on the grass, gazing up at the full moon. She often remained there until Elijah came to find her when the sun rose.

"Is this where you come to sulk?" asked a high-pitched female voice.

Riley huffed and turned to see Latavia.

Latavia's pale face was devoid of makeup and she was dressed in a worn track suit. Her usually immaculate hair had been pulled back into a messy bun.

Riley was too tired to come up with a decent jab at the other woman's sloppy appearance.

"You're up early?" Riley muttered.

"Of course I am," Latavia snapped back. "I have a fucking newborn, you idiot."

"Isn't there some old lady that you can hand it off to?"

"Not when they can use my body to save money on formula."

"Guess they'd rather put it towards their next mansion."

"Bingo," said Latavia. "Maybe you're not so stupid for a muncher after all."

Riley let out a sigh of frustration and got to her feet. She'd come to relax, not get into another pointless argument with Latavia.

A small plastic box landed before Riley's feet.

"What's this?" Riley asked.

"Just those pills that you munchers love."

"Seriously?" Riley quickly scooped up the container and popped it open, surprised to see over twenty white pills.

"They probably sent your son to a colony a few hours south," said Latavia. "It's where they usually dump all the munchers and half-breeds. Just follow the highway until the scent of muncher hits you."

"Why?" Riley closed the box and slipped it into her pocket. "Why are you doing this?"

"Because I want him to suffer."

"Who?"

"Elijah, of course, you dipshit," Latavia spat. "Everyone seems to have forgotten, but we were together for years until he met you."

"Oh."

"He promised to always support me and stay by my side, but he fucked off the moment that you showed up."

Riley didn't know what to say. It was easy to pass Latavia off as an entitled bitch, but she was used and disappointed by the people around her.

"He doesn't deserve to be happy," Latavia said.

Those words caused a pang in Riley's chest, but she quickly brushed it away. "Thanks for this."

"Don't thank me," Latavia snapped and turned to leave. "Just get the fuck out of here and never come back."

Riley swallowed three pills the moment that she returned home. She couldn't wait. Her anxious body itched with the urge to get out of the settlement.

There was a small map slipped in amongst the pills, outlining an old highway on the other side of the mountains.

Muncher truckers pass through here, was written in Latavia's neat handwriting.

Riley went to the laundry and stuffed several shirts and pants into one of Elijah's backpacks, followed by three energy bars and a loaf of bread from the kitchen.

The ceiling creaked above her.

Riley froze.

She waited for Elijah's footsteps down the hall, but all was silent.

Riley let out a sigh of relief. She stuffed more food into her backpack, then slipped out of the house.

Riley dashed through the dark forest in wolf form, using the light from the moon and the surrounding mountains to guide her way.

As the adrenaline wore off, her doubts began to creep in.

Could she really do it? Could she really leave Elijah forever?

He wasn't so bad. He seemed to love her and treated her well. Riley felt an intense connection with him that she'd never experienced before. Perhaps they could even be happy together.

But Ryan would never be part of that picture.

She knew that Ryan and their future children would be sent away to be indoctrinated and raised by the cult's elderly leaders, encouraged to breed and produce countless children of their own.

If the next baby was a girl, there was no way of knowing if she'd be treated any better than Wanda or Latavia. They'd have a life of being passed around various men and forced to give birth until they became angry and bitter.

Riley refused to let that happen. She needed to leave for the sake of her unborn child.

The first rays of dawn illuminated the horizon as Riley reached the highway. There were cracks in the concrete and the paint had long faded, but she felt hope for the first time in weeks.

Riley transformed back to her human form. She slipped the backpack off her shoulders and pulled out a shirt, jeans, and shoes, quickly putting them on.

Just a little longer.

She planned to hitchhike on the first truck and be back in human civilization by noon. From there she could work on a plan to find Ryan. She could have her old life back by the end of the week.

Riley took a seat on a piece of bent railing by the side of the road.

All she had to do was wait.

CHAPTER TEN

Latavia must have been fucking with her.

The sun was up and Riley had been waiting for over two hours, but not a single truck went past.

The road was clearly neglected from disuse. The metal railings were rusted and weeds poked up from the cracks in the road. It didn't look like it had been maintained for years.

Riley felt the bottom drop from her stomach.

What if no one was coming?

It wouldn't take long for Elijah to notice her missing. He'd soon come looking and drag her back to the settlement to be tied down and bred. There was no way that he would let her out of his sight again.

"*Fuck*," Riley hissed and anxiously scratched her arm, leaving red marks.

She jogged down the road, unsure if it was the right way, but she needed to move. If no one was coming, then she'd find a way out herself.

A large white wolf dashed out before Riley, blocking her way.

Riley screamed and fell back.

The white wolf transformed into Elijah. His naked chest rapidly heaved up and down like he'd been sprinting for miles.

"Riley," he huffed, voice laced with desperation. "What are you doing?"

"No!" Riley cried and shook her head. "I'm not going back."

"But it's our home." He extended his hand. "Come back with me."

Riley hesitated. It would be easy to give in and go back to the life they had created together, but if she didn't leave now, then she knew she never would.

"No!" Riley yelled at him. "I'm not going back there!"

"Please," Elijah begged and followed after her. "Don't be so immature. You'll only just transform and come back on your own."

"No, not this time!"

"But we're fated mates!"

"No! Fuck your fated mates shit!" The urge to unleash weeks of pent-up anguish was overwhelming. "That's just an excuse you use to justify your own messed up crap."

"But I can feel it." He placed a hand on his chest. "It led me here straight to you."

"But that doesn't make me your slave," Riley cried back. "All we ever do is what you want! What about me and my needs? A relationship is supposed to be a two-way street, Elijah."

"I provide for your needs! I'll give you anything that you want."

"Really? Then let me leave!"

Elijah let out a sigh of frustration. "You know that I can't do that."

"Why the fuck not?"

"Because I've told you a hundred times. My life is here. They need me here."

"They don't need you," Riley spat. "All your grandfather needs is an obedient little dog to carry out his dirty work. You don't even get to see your own children."

"But things can change, Grandfather said-"

"Wake the fuck up, Elijah!" Riley yelled, hands shaking with rage. "Your grandfather is never going to give you what you want. He just dangles it in front of your face like a carrot to keep you in line. We're never going to see Ryan! And the next kid will be taken away too."

Elijah appeared stunned. "You don't know that," he muttered.

"Well... I'm not hanging around to find out." Riley turned and started walking away, hoping that her words were enough to discourage him. "Unlike you, I'm taking charge of my life."

"We'll see!" he called after her. "You'll be back in my bed by sundown!"

"Not this time, motherfucker!" she said, giving him the finger.

Riley realized that she'd made a mistake when Elijah rushed after her.

He wrapped his large arms around her waist, pulling her to his chest and inhaling her scent. "Where did you get those?"

"Stop it!" Riley struggled out of his hold. "How does it matter?"

"Who gave you that poison?" He reached for her backpack and tugged at the zip.

"Just stop it!" Riley cried, shoving him away. "Just....let me leave...."

"No." Elijah shook his head. "You can't leave." He reached for her, pulling Riley tightly to his chest. "Don't leave me like that again."

Riley struggled against his grasp. It was difficult to breathe. "Stop it.... just let me go."

"No." Elijah shook his head. "We belong together."

"Please," Riley begged. Her face felt numb as tears leaked from her eyes. "Don't take me back to that place. Don't let them take my children away."

"We'll make it work," said Elijah. "I'll talk to the elders and-"

"I'd rather kill myself." Riley was shocked by her own words. "I'd rather kill myself then let them have any more of my children."

"Please don't say that." Elijah trembled. "Please don't say things like that."

"I don't belong there," Riley sobbed. "They all hate me. Every second I stay, I feel like I'm going mad."

Elijah gripped her tighter. "I'll find a way."

"There is no way! What are the two of us going to do against all of them? What if the baby is a girl? What if they take her, and use her, and I never get to see her again?"

Elijah nodded like he knew she was right.

"Just please let me go," Riley sobbed, looking up to see tears running down Elijah's face. "Please do it for their sake."

Elijah went silent. His broad shoulders shook as he nuzzled her head. "*Okay*," he whispered.

"Okay what?"

"*I'll leave.*"

"Seriously?" Riley felt Elijah's hold relax. She pulled away. "You'll do that?"

Elijah wiped his face with the back of his hand. "Yeah, let's do it." He took a deep breath and tried to compose himself. "We'll try doing things your way this time."

Riley couldn't contain a smile. "That's great. I-"

"But there's one condition," said Elijah. "If things don't work out, I need you to promise that you'll come back here with me."

"Okay." Riley was unsure if it was wise to agree, but she was willing to take a chance. "Let's do it."

A small white truck appeared an hour later.

Riley immediately waved it down.

The driver was an elderly man in his seventies. His green eyes roamed over the large pink blouse and blue skirt that Elijah was wearing.

"Rough night?" asked the driver.

"You wouldn't believe it," Riley smiled. "We were hiking and our group left without us."

"Hiking in a skirt?" he said while staring at Elijah's girly outfit. "With no shoes?"

"Guys are dicks, right?" Riley laughed. "They stole his clothes, so I had to lend him some of mine."

The driver rolled his eyes and gestured to the passenger seat. "Hop on in."

Riley climbed up into the truck, followed by Elijah.

"Not many folks up here these days," said the driver as he pulled out onto the road. "Not since they built the tunnel."

"Except you," said Riley.

"Just me....and the crazies who live over the mountain," laughed the old man. "Good thing you didn't run into them."

Elijah threaded his fingers through Riley's, tightly gripping her hand.

He silently stared out the window, but Riley could feel the anxiety rolling off him in waves.

She didn't know where they were heading, or if she'd find Ryan, but for the first time in months, she felt hope.

Riley knew that finding happiness with Elijah wouldn't be easy. Their relationship was messed up and there was still so much she didn't understand about the bond between them. Learning to peacefully live together wouldn't be easy, but she wanted to try.

Perhaps one day she'd even feel comfortable calling him her fated mate.

Thank you for reading "Werewolf Breeding Academy."

Enjoy a free bonus chapter that shows Riley and Elijah a year after they escape!

books.beatrixarden.com/werewolfbonus

SUBSCRIBE TO
BEATRIX ARDEN

  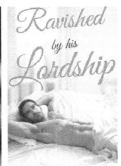

ALSO BY BEATRIX ARDEN

Find more hot stories by Beatrix Arden at

www.beatrixarden.com

You're my Omega

Alpha girl Sara discovers that her school enemy is secretly an Omega. When he suddenly goes into heat and begs her to mate him, she finds it impossible to resist.

omega.beatrixarden.com

Omega Harem Lost

Omegaverse story. Kana is tasked with waiting on a warlord's Omega. When Kana suddenly presents as an Omega herself, the two only have each other for heat.

harem.beatrixarden.com

Chained Omega

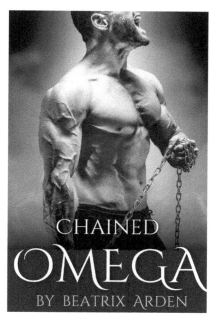

Omega Franklin lives in a world where Alphas are extinct, but that doesn't stop him from buying one for his bed.

Franklin thinks that he's in control.....until he suddenly isn't.

chained.beatrixarden.com